A CHRISTMAS TO REMEMBER

By DENISE DEVINE
USA TODAY Bestselling Author

A Christmas to Remember

Copyright 2015 by Denise Devine

www.deniseannettedevine.com

Large Print Edition

ISBN: 978-0-9915956-4-8

This story is a work of fiction. Names, characters, places and incidents are either products of the author's imagination or used fictitiously. Any resemblance of actual events, locales or persons, living or dead, is entirely coincidental.

All rights reserved.

No part of this publication may be reproduced or transmitted in any form or by any means, electronic or mechanical, including photocopying, recording, or by any information storage or retrieval system, without the written permission of Denise Devine, except short excerpts for reviews. Published in the United States of America

Cover art by Shelley Schmidt

To Jill, Lori, LuAnn, Shelley, Stacey and Tracey
Girls just want to write fun!

USA Today Bestselling Author

Kindle Top 100 Bestselling Author

"This writer never disappoints."

~ Christine Arness

"Ms. Devine's characters will leave you laughing and begging for more."

~ Nancy Schumacher, Sr. Editor, Satin Romance

Chapter One

Katie McGowan considered herself a pretty good driver. At thirty-three, she'd seen her share of bad weather, but she'd never experienced anything like *this*. The storm started out as a steady drizzle soon after she left Fargo on I-94 East, heading back to Minneapolis. Once the blustery Canadian winds began to push into Minnesota, the drizzle turned to sleet then became a rippling curtain of solid white, limiting her visibility to the taillights on the vehicle ahead of her. The slippery conditions and blowing snow forced her to reduce her speed to forty miles per hour.

The Malibu began to slide toward the shoulder, as though being pushed by an invisible force. Snow scraped the underside of her car, causing her to grip the wheel with white knuckled hands. Slowly, she straightened the front wheels and steered back into the grooves carved by the huge tires of the monstrous pickup truck ahead of her.

"Why do we have to get a big snowstorm on the same day I'm driving back to Minneapolis," Katie complained aloud, her heart pounding like a jackhammer as she peered through the flapping windshield wipers. "This is going to mess up my holiday plans."

She'd spent the last four days in Fargo, North Dakota, at the new branch office of Prairie Star Newspapers, reviewing the benefits package with each employee and completing the paperwork. On Friday morning, she left early to get ahead of the storm, but it quickly caught up with her. She'd planned to spend the weekend with her parents and get into the Christmas mood by watching classic holiday movies and helping her mom bake an assortment of cookies. Mom and Dad were expecting her for dinner tonight at six o'clock, but the way things looked now, she might not make it back to Minneapolis until very late.

Oh, well, she thought, *I'll catch up on sleep after Christmas.*

Buried deep in her purse, her phone began to ring, but she let it go to voicemail and concentrated on her driving. She couldn't even glance away from the road much less reach across the seat and dig into her bag.

Through the blowing snow, she spied a large green sign that read "Alexandria, Exit 100" and let out a small cheer. Luckily, the truck ahead of her drove up the exit first and plowed a path. At the top of the ramp, she stared through the swirling cloud wondering which way to go. Though she knew the city of Alexandria well, the whiteout conditions disoriented her, causing her to lose all sense of direction. She desperately needed to find a gas station where she could pull in temporarily and call home.

At the top of the exit, the truck turned right. She glanced around, surveying her limited options. To her left, the road looked impassable, covered with at least a foot of snow. She decided to play it safe and follow the truck.

Straight ahead, Katie saw a snowplowing contractor clearing the parking lot of a large gas station. Breathing a sigh of relief, she veered her car onto the frontage road and drove to the station.

Her phone began ringing again. She parked under the shelter of the station's canopy and tore through her purse. The caller ID displayed *Prairie Star Newspapers*. "Hello?"

"Katie, where are you? I've been trying to reach you for over an hour! Are you okay?"

"I've got a major case of the shakes, but other than that, I'm fine," she said to Marcey, the Executive Assistant to the Director of Human Resources at the newspaper office. "I'm in Minnesota now at a gas station in Alexandria. The snow is coming down so fast I can hardly see to drive, much less answer calls. How's the weather in Minneapolis?"

"I'm so glad you're all right! It's starting to sleet here and the snow isn't far behind," Marcey said. "According to the weatherman, MNDOT is closing down I-94 at Alexandria because the wind is creating impossible driving conditions. You escaped just in time. The barricades are going up right now and the Highway Patrol is directing people off the freeway. It looks like you're going to be spending the night there, but don't worry, I'm looking for a hotel room for you."

Katie gripped the phone. Spend the night here? No way! "Marcey, I can't stay in Alexandria tonight.

Tomorrow is Christmas Eve! Mom and Dad are expecting me for dinner and I have to stop at my apartment first to pick up gifts."

"Hold on," Marcey said, ignoring her plea. Marcey went silent except for the clickety-click of her typing. "Katie, I have a list of accommodations for the area and I'm working my way through it. I'd better get back to calling before everything fills up. Sit tight. I'll call you back as soon as I can."

"Marcey, wait—" The line went dead.

Katie tossed her phone on the seat and stared out the window. This couldn't be happening. She had to get home tonight!

Her stomach rumbled, prompting her to dig through her bag for something to snack on. She'd missed lunch an hour ago, so a Snickers bar and a half-empty bag of strawberry Twizzlers would have to do. She bit into a Twizzler stick and called her mother. No one answered. She tried her father's cell phone. That rang repeatedly, too.

"Where are they," she said aloud in frustration, chewing on a mouthful of candy. Her parents had a bad habit of forgetting their cell phones at home or simply not hearing the phones ring if they were watching the news. Over the years, her father had gradually lost his hearing in one ear, but rather than wear a hearing aid, he preferred to crank up the volume instead. They were probably sitting in front of the TV right now, getting the latest updates on the weather and wondering why she hadn't called.

The call went to voicemail. "Hi, Dad," Katie said, "this is the first chance I've had to check my missed calls this morning. Don't worry. I'm okay. I made it as far as Alexandria, but it looks like I'm stuck here overnight because the Highway Patrol is closing down the freeway. My boss' assistant is booking a room for me right now. Tell Mom I'm sorry I can't make it for dinner. I'll call her when I reach the hotel. Bye."

Katie disconnected the call and sat brooding. She didn't want to stay here overnight. She didn't want to be stuck in this town! Reaching into her bag, she pulled out the Snickers bar. When upset, eat chocolate!

I need to get back on that freeway and be on my way.

A couple minutes later, Marcey rang her back.

"I've got good news and bad news," Marcey

said. "Which one do you want first?"

"I could use some good news about now."

"Right! The good news is, I found you a first-rate hotel and the only rooms left were the king suites, so you're going to spend the night getting the royal treatment."

"What's so bad about that?" Katie stuffed the last bite of the Snickers bar in her mouth.

She heard Marcey draw in a deep breath. "...it's at Lakewood Resort."

The candy bar stuck in her throat like a glob of sugary cement. She swallowed hard. "I *can't* stay there. You know that. Please find me something else."

"Believe me, I would if I could," Marcey said, her voice threaded with regret. "I'm sorry, Katie, but that's the only hotel left with anything available in the entire city. All of the less expensive accommodations went first and the others filled up after that. There were only two suites left at the resort when I called and the other one is most likely gone by now, too."

Katie's heart began to slam in her chest. "I-I

can't do this. You know that's where...where Josh..."

The scene came back with startling clarity; the grinding howl of snowmobile engines, the explosive crash of metal on metal, the screams...Josh airborne then his lifeless body crumpled in the snow...

"I know it's hard to go back to the place where Josh was...had his accident, Katie, but you have no other choice."

"I have an emergency kit in my trunk. I could pull into another hotel parking lot and keep the car running to stay warm."

"Katie, that's unthinkable! What will you do to keep warm once the gas runs out? And that's not your only problem."

Distracted by the crash scene blaring loudly in her head, Katie barely heard what Marcey said. "What do you mean?"

"What will you do when you have to use the bathroom?"

The words "use the bathroom" forced her to focus. It would be tough to sit in a cold car with no food, watching the snow pile up as her only entertainment, but the thought of not having any "facilities," as her dad would say, gave her pause. A hot shower and something good to eat sounded wonderful right now, just not at Lakewood Resort!

"You *can* do this, Katie. It has been two years since you've last seen the place." Marcey paused, as if to give her a chance to think it over. "Maybe going back there is just what you need."

Though Marcey would never be tactless enough to say the words, the implication of what she really meant came across loud and clear. *Going back to Lakewood Resort will force you to face Josh's death, finally, and move on with your life.*

No way, Katie thought stubbornly. She'd vowed never to come back to Lakewood Resort because it had caused her too much pain. *I don't want to deal with that now—or ever.*

A sudden gust of wind rocked the Malibu. She checked the gas gauge. The needle pointed to the halfway mark. One-half of a tank would not last long in this weather. She could brave the storm and fill up here, but even a full tank wouldn't get her through the night. She stared across the parking lot, knowing she had to get going and the longer she procrastinated, the worse it would be once she got back on the road. The area the snowplow had cleared already had an accumulation of new snow.

Katie let out a deep breath. "Marcey, are you still there?"

"Of course I am. I'm not hanging up until you promise me you're going to take that room at the Lakewood Resort and be safe."

She went silent for a few moments, mulling it over. "This is not fair," she said in a grumbling voice. "I'll drive over there and give it a try, but I'm not guaranteeing I'll stay."

"Wonderful! Do you need directions?"

"No. I'll use my cell phone GPS."

"Great! Look, I have the weather report on my monitor and you need to leave *now*. This storm is turning into a slow-moving blizzard and the longer you wait, the more dangerous it's becoming. Get going before the police have to form a search party to find you."

"Okay," Katie said, becoming alarmed at the prospect of getting lost or worse, ending up in the ditch. "The Lakewood Resort can't be far from here, but I have no idea what condition the roads are in over there by Lake Darling."

"Drive carefully and call me as soon as you arrive. If I don't hear from you in twenty minutes, I'm going to call 911!"

Katie hung up and got busy pulling up the directions on her phone. As soon as she drove out of the lot and turned onto the main road, her car began to slide, but she reduced her speed and kept moving. She drove toward the freeway and risked a glance as she passed the northbound on-ramp, hoping the Highway Patrol hadn't closed the barrier yet.

She gasped when she saw red and blue flashing lights from a half-dozen squad cars on the freeway below. It looked like a semi-truck and trailer had jackknifed across the southbound lanes. Vehicles filled both sides of the ditch like piles of snow-covered dominoes. Headlights beamed like beacons through the blowing snow from cars lined up waiting to be detoured onto the exit ramp once the tow trucks had cleared through the drifts to open a temporary lane. Frightened, she focused straight ahead and kept on going, passing a roadblock of police cars closing off the southbound entrance to the freeway.

The GPS led her across town, directing her

turn by turn until she reached Lakewood Lane, but she couldn't let her guard down until she drove through the guest parking lot into the circular entrance at the Lakewood Resort and Conference Center.

Her stomach fluttered with dread. The last time she had stayed here, she'd departed in an ambulance with Josh and never returned. She'd buried him a few days later, exactly two weeks before Christmas. Thankfully, she'd had the love and support of her parents to help her get through the holiday that year and every year since. She couldn't imagine spending Christmas without them.

She slid to a stop under the porte cochére and stared at the massive brick and stucco building. Pine boughs, red velvet ribbon and multi-colored lights dressed the large windows spanning the front. A pair of snow-covered wreaths hung on the double doors of the entrance. The bell captain came out to greet her, dressed in a black jacket and fur cap. A gust of icy wind and snow swirled around her as she lowered the window, causing her to shiver.

"We're fully booked, Ma'am, but due to the blizzard we're allowing people to take shelter in the lobby. Do you have a reservation?" The nametag on his jacket read "Ron."

"Yes, I do," Katie shouted, squinting to avoid getting snow in her eyes.

"May I assist with your luggage?"

She pressed the trunk release. "I have one bag."

"Just give the bell desk a call when you get into your room and we'll deliver it." Ron handed her a ticket for the suitcase and pointed toward the guest parking lot. "You'll have to find a spot in the open area, I'm afraid. Valet parking is full."

She raised the window and waited for him to remove her bag then stepped on the gas. But the car didn't move forward. Instead, the front wheels spun on a patch of ice, making a loud whining noise. Then the car simply slid sideways.

Ron reappeared at her window. "The valet can give you a push. Unfortunately, I only have one on duty today and he's busy helping someone else right now, so you'll have to wait your turn. When he comes back, I'll have him assist you."

A horn blast forced her to turn around and look

through the back window. Several cars had lined up behind her, waiting for her to drive on so they could drop off passengers and bags under the shelter of the canopy. The guy behind her made a rude gesture and laid on his horn again.

Katie leaned her forehead against the steering wheel and groaned. Could this day get any worse?

Chapter Two

Ryan Scott sat at the Eagle's Nest bar in the Lakewood Resort and nursed a cold beer while he stared idly at a basketball game on the sports channel. A heavy-set bartender with curly red hair and matching beard stood on the other side of the counter, attempting to coax small talk out of him. The nametag pinned to his long-sleeved navy polo read "Red."

"How about this weather? Gonna be nice cruising on a fast sled once the wind dies down."

"Yep." Ryan took a sip of his beer and watched seven-foot basketball players dancing across the TV screen.

"You own one?"

Ryan pulled his attention from the game long enough to glance at the guy. "Snowmobile? Yep."

Red leaned against the bar with his palms spread on the counter. "Whatcha got?"

"Polaris Rush."

"Uh-huh." The bartender grinned, his deep blue eyes sparkling at the mention of a Polaris. "So, you like trails."

"Pretty much, yeah." Ryan didn't mean to be rude, but no way did he feel like making frivolous chitchat. He'd come up here from Minneapolis to be alone for a few days and deal with the shock of his parents' sudden, vitriolic divorce. Their decision to cancel the family Christmas gathering and instead leave town on separate vacations had deeply hurt his sister. It simply angered him. His parents had put up with each other for the last forty years. Why couldn't they have stuck it out two more weeks for their family's sake? He understood why they'd decided to split up, but disagreed with their timing.

I'm never getting married. If it has to end like this, who needs it?

Ignoring his moodiness, Red reached under the counter and pulled out a glass bowl of snack mix, setting it in front of Ryan. "Are you stranded by the blizzard or staying here for the holidays?"

"Both."

Red looked puzzled. "Huh?"

Ryan drained the last of his beer and pushed the bottle away. "If it wasn't for the fact that you can't see your hand in front of your face, I'd be out on my sled right now." Across the room, a two-story wall of windows provided a magnificent panorama of the lake, but today the view amounted to a swirling cloud of white. "Until the storm lets up, I'm sitting around, wasting a perfectly good weekend."

"Bored, huh?"

"You could say that."

A gray-haired guy walked into the bar, late fifties, dressed in a purple and gold jacket with the Minnesota Vikings logo on the chest. He stopped next to Ryan, but his attention focused on Red. "Hey, there's a woman outside in a blue Malibu who could use a push," he announced loudly. "She slid on some ice and now she's blocking the entrance."

Ryan slid off the barstool and grabbed his jacket, eager to answer the call. He didn't much care for the idea of pushing a car through a blizzard, but it sure beat sitting here while Red pestered him with a million pointless questions. He jammed his arms into his jacket and started for the door. No one followed, not even the guy who asked for volunteers. *Whatever*. Given his present mood, he didn't need any help.

~*~

Katie sat in her car and fought back tears of frustration. She'd been driving for nearly four hours without incident in rain, sleet and blowing snow, only to get her car hung up on a stupid patch of ice—right in front of the resort!

Where is that valet? I've been holding up the line for almost ten minutes, she thought miserably, swallowing back a lump in her throat.

Someone rapped on the driver's side window and she nearly jumped out of her skin. She didn't see anyone approach the car and the sharp tapping on the glass took her by surprise. A tall, broad-shouldered man with thick, dark hair, wearing a red and black jacket leaned sideways, peering through the glass. She lowered the window. Bone-chilling wind and snow blew in her face. "If you're stuck behind me, I'm sorry. My car won't move."

He studied her with intense brown eyes. "Actually, I'm here to help you." His deep voice held a note of authority.

"Are you the valet?"

He shook his head. "Someone in the bar said you were stuck on a patch of ice."

Her mood went from zero to sixty in the space of a sentence. Glory halleluiah! She smiled and blinked back the moisture in her eyes. She needed to get a good look at her handsome hero. "Yes, thank you so much! I really appreciate your coming out to assist me."

"Are you leaving or trying to move your car into the guest lot?" He said, getting down to business.

"I'm not going anywhere but to the closest parking spot available!"

He looked relieved. "Okay. When I shout, give the car a little gas. I'll do the rest." He walked to the back of the car and bent low, bracing his hands against the deck lid of the trunk. "Ready? Go!"

Katie pressed lightly on the gas pedal. The front wheels began to spin again, but the car started moving forward, inching little by little over the ice until the vehicle broke free and lurched ahead. She drove into the guest lot and slowly made her way toward what looked like the only parking spot left. The man stood at the driver's side door, opening it for her before she pulled the key out of the ignition.

"Thank you for helping me out," she repeated as he took her hand and steadied her while she climbed out of the car.

"Do you need help with your bags?"

"I only had a small one and it's at the bell station already. I'm just an accidental tourist. As soon as this storm blows through, I'm out of here. I need to get home by tomorrow. My mother is planning a huge Christmas Eve dinner and I don't want to miss it." Once the words came out, she blushed with embarrassment. She had no idea what prompted her to tell him all of that.

For a fleeting moment, sadness clouded his eyes. Then he blinked, as if to dismiss the thought and replaced the expression with a slight grin. "Okay, Ms. Accidental Tourist. I hope you get your grownup Christmas wish."

Katie started to smile. Without thinking, she innocently glanced at the Polaris logo on the front of the man's jacket. Josh had worn a Polaris jacket the day he died. Her momentary happiness turned into confusion as her knees buckled.

"Whoa," he said, sounding surprised once he realized she'd collapsed. He wrapped his arms around her and hauled her to her feet, catching her just before her backside hit the snow. "Are you okay?"

His long arms circling her waist caught her off guard, holding her with surprising gentleness as he pulled her close. She looked up, her hood falling back on her shoulders. Staring into his deep brown eyes, she forgot about the similarity of his jacket; her mind suddenly went blank... "I—I think so."

He gently pulled her hood back over her head. "You're getting covered with snow. We'd better get inside." He hooked his arm in hers and together they tromped through the drifts.

At the entrance, Katie stopped. "Did you hear that?"

He looked puzzled. "Hear what?"

She scanned the snow-covered sidewalk, but only saw a cement bench and a large, square planter holding a small Christmas tree decorated with blue lights. "I could swear it sounded like a whimper."

"You mean, like a child's voice?" Concerned, he turned around and inspected the immediate area. "I don't see anything. It must be the wind."

The doorman, a tall, stately man in a long dark coat and wool cap, opened a wreath-covered door and smiled. "Greetings. Welcome to the Lakewood Resort." He stood aside for them to enter.

They crossed the threshold of the busy lobby, overflowing with luggage and people stranded by the storm. The clamor of voices and piped in music playing, "Let It Snow! Let It Snow! Let It Snow!" filled the air. The lobby resembled a huge living room with wooden beams framing the vaulted ceiling, a towering Christmas tree decorated with shiny ornaments and twinkling lights, and in the center of the room, a massive stone fireplace hosting a crackling fire. People clustered on the leather sofas and easy chairs around the fire, chatting or scrolling the Internet on their phones. Some children played on the polished wood floor, preoccupied with their toys while others chased each other around, laughing and playing tag.

Katie drew in a sharp breath, her heart flooding with painful memories of her last hours in this hotel.

Oh, how she missed Josh!

I need to get out of here, she thought desperately. *I can't breathe with so many memories bombarding me, reminding me of how much I miss him.*

Marcey's urgent plea replayed in her head. *You can do this, Katie...*

No, I can't!

You can do this, Katie!

Her temporary companion interrupted her thoughts with a concerned look. "Are you feeling all right? Your face is as white as the snow flying outside."

"I-I'm fine. I just need to sit for a minute." She allowed him to guide her to a vacant bench near the fireplace.

"I'll be right back." He sprinted to the VIP line at the registration area and grabbed a complimentary bottle of water off the counter. "Here," he said and tore the cap off the bottle once he rejoined her. "Drink this and try to relax. Driving in this storm is enough to make anyone a nervous wreck."

She obediently took a couple swallows of the

cool water.

He squatted beside her. "Feel better now?"

She nodded. "A little."

He rose and smiled warmly. "If I don't see you again, have a great holiday."

"Th-thanks. You, too."

Katie didn't know if she simply liked his handsome smile, or because being around him distracted her from thinking about the last time she'd been in this resort, but she suddenly didn't want to let him go. She stood up and extended her hand. "I'm Katie, by the way. Katie McGowan."

"It was a pleasure to meet you, Katie. I'm Ryan Scott."

An awkward silence settled between them as they stood, shaking hands. She sensed he wanted to say more, but had the distinct feeling something held him back. Perhaps he had girlfriend—or wife—waiting for him and didn't want to be more than a helpful stranger.

A raucous cheer echoed from The Eagle's Nest Bar on the upper level. He glanced toward the noise.

"I'd better get back to the game," he said

lightly and dropped her hand. "Good night." He waived goodbye and walked away.

Katie drew in a deep breath to muster her courage and slowly made her way to the line of people waiting in the registration area. When she looked back, Ryan Scott had disappeared.

Chapter Three

"Next! I can help the next person in line!"

Katie inched forward as the man ahead of her headed toward the next available registration clerk to check in. She'd been standing in line for nearly a half-hour, waiting her turn. During that time, she'd called her mother to assure her parents she'd found a room and made it safely to the hotel. Then she called Marcey back as well.

Behind her, a hotel employee worked his way up the line, handing out complimentary treats. "Would you like a sugar cookie and some cider? How about a gingerbread man?" He paused at Katie, ignoring her refusal. "Oh, come on, take one. They're fresh out of the oven."

Katie selected one and helped herself to a juice-sized glass of warm cider. "This is my third Christmas cookie, you know. I've consumed enough sugar today to fuel a rocket to Mars." A couple people in line chuckled. She broke a piece off the soft, frosted snowman and chewed it slowly. What she really needed was a decent meal. By the time she got into her room it would be almost the dinner hour.

"Next! I can help the next person in line!"

Someone nudged her. "Hey, it's your turn."

When she looked up, she saw a female clerk waving at her. She walked swiftly to the registration counter, her gray wool coat and striped scarf draped over her arm. "Hi, my name is Katie McGowan, M-C-G-O-W-A-N."

The clerk spent a minute typing on her computer. "For two nights?"

"No, I just need tonight."

The woman stared at her. "I have you down for a king suite which has a minimum requirement of two nights prepaid."

Katie shrugged. "Okay, but I'm only staying until the storm is over so I'm probably leaving tomorrow morning."

The woman gave her a wry look, as if to suggest she should get real and accept the fact that the weather had sabotaged everyone's holiday plans. Katie refrained from commenting and let it go. She *had* to leave tomorrow; she had to be back in Minneapolis by Christmas Eve.

Fifteen minutes later, she slipped the key card into the door of her room and walked into a spacious suite with a plush sofa, king-sized bed, a wet bar and a sixty-inch TV. She stood in the middle of the room and stared at the furnishings—the same furniture, drapes and color scheme of the suite she and Josh had occupied on their last stay here—their honeymoon. Memories of the last night in their suite washed over her, stinging her eyes with tears and forcing her to ask herself the same question she'd asked herself a million times. Why did this senseless tragedy have to happen to him?

I have to get out of here, but where do I go? Everywhere I turn, reminders of Josh, and what I've lost forever are all around me.

The stress of the day had taken its toll, leaving her depressed and exhausted. She dropped her purse, coat and scarf on the floor and sank down on the sofa, wiping away persistent tears. Truthfully, she was too weary to think about driving home tomorrow, too emotionally drained to reflect any longer on Josh's accident. Sick and tired of struggling to push her last night with Josh from her mind.

She ran her hands through her hair and stared at the ceiling. Now what? Perhaps a hot shower would clear her mind and relax her body so she could go to sleep, but she remembered she needed to call the bell desk and have her suitcase delivered first. Then her stomach growled, promptly reminding her she hadn't eaten a decent meal all day. She briefly considered ordering room service, but decided against it. She needed something to eat *now*. She needed to get out of this room *now*.

With a loud groan, Katie dragged herself off the sofa and grabbed her purse, ready to go searching for something to eat.

~*~

Ryan sat at the bar, trying to concentrate on the basketball game, but it didn't hold his interest anymore. His mind kept drifting back to Katie McGowan, Ms. Accidental Tourist. Darn, she was cute, especially those big blue eyes. He'd always been partial to petite blondes with long hair and a beautiful smile, and from the moment he'd pulled her into his arms out there in the snowy parking lot, she'd been on his mind.

Nice girl, lousy timing...

With so much going on in his personal life, he hesitated to get involved with anyone. He didn't want people outside of his immediate family exposed to the knock-down-drag-out mess his parents had created. Their relationship had always been stormy, so the dissolution of their marriage and the complicated negotiations of their property settlement promised to generate plenty of drama. Ryan hated family strife and tried to avoid it at all costs. Unfortunately, he and his sister worked at their family-owned Mercedes dealership, making it impossible to escape the nuclear war between his parents in the days to come.

Besides, he reasoned, Katie probably already had a guy or two in her life. A girl as eye-catching as her would have men falling all over themselves to ask her out.

But then...why did she give him an indication back there in the lobby that she wanted to get to know him better?

He shook his head. *Let it go. You're not looking for an entanglement. You came up here to escape Christmas, to get away from the family drama and enjoy some fast rides on your sled.*

He turned and gazed out the windows at the heavy, blowing snow. When this storm moved on, the trails would be pristine with deep powder snow, but when would the raging wind end? Restless, he drank the rest of his beer and grabbed his coat.

"Taking off?" Red the bartender gave him a quizzical look.

Ryan pushed a couple dollars toward the man. "I'm going outside to check on the weather. See you later."

In the lobby, he looked through the front doors and saw the bell captain outside in the dark, smoking a cigarette. He zipped his jacket and went out to join the guy.

"What's it like out here, Ron?" he asked, reading Ron's nametag. "Any chance the storm is winding down yet?"

Ron shook his head and flicked the ashes on his cigarette. "No, if anything it's getting worse. I hear we could get up to twenty-four inches before it's all over."

Then he heard it—a whimper so faint he wondered if he'd merely mistaken it for the wind again.

Ron didn't seem to notice as he tapped his boot to Bing Crosby's "It's Beginning to Look a Lot Like Christmas" coming from a speaker concealed somewhere around the entrance.

Ryan pulled up the collar on his jacket and shoved his hands into his gloves. "I can't wait to get my sled out on the trails."

"Yeah, I'll bet you're chomping at the bit with all this new powder coming down."

"Well, I came here to hit the trails this weekend, but so far I haven't even had a chance to roll the sled out of the trailer."

The whimper sounded again, this time louder.

Ryan spun around. "Did you hear that?"

Ron shrugged. "Hear what?"

"It sounded like a whining noise." Ryan pointed toward the large cement planter in the inside corner of the entrance area. "It might have come from over there."

Ron walked over to the planter and looked

down. "There's the culprit."

Ryan followed him and saw a medium-sized black dog, completely covered in long, wavy hair, huddled on a small mat behind the planter. Sad, round eyes stared up at him.

Ron flicked his cigarette into the ash can. "I told the valets to stop coddling this mutt. It's bad enough the housekeepers and the waitstaff won't quit feeding it. I'll have to report this." He gave the dog a shove with his foot. "Get out of here!"

The furry dog yelped and ran away, scurrying down the sidewalk toward the end of the building.

Horrified, Ryan turned toward Ron. "Hey, what'd you do that for? It wasn't hurting anyone by hiding back there. It just wanted to protect itself from the wind."

Ron opened the door and held it for Ryan to enter. "We can't allow strays to hang around the front entrance and beg for food. It's the management's rule, not mine."

Ryan took one last look in the direction the dog ran, but couldn't see it anywhere. Not knowing what else to do, he followed Ron back into the building.

They parted ways and Ryan stood smoldering in the lobby. How could that guy be so heartless? The poor dog couldn't help being homeless. The memory of those sad eyes haunted him. It wouldn't last out in the elements without shelter or food. He wondered what to do.

A pair of young boys walked past him, each holding a hot dog. The spicy aroma filled his nostrils, giving him an idea.

"Hey, there, junior, where did you get that?"

A tow-headed boy stopped and pointed toward the snack bar, located at the other end of the lobby. "It cost a dollar," he said through a mouthful of food.

Ryan hustled over to the snack bar and bought two hot dogs. He grabbed the sack and headed back outside. No one had shoveled the sidewalk in a while, making it easy for him to follow the dog's tracks. He reached the corner of the building and followed the markings in the snow to a large pickup truck. Getting down on his knees, he peered under the truck and found the dog huddled behind one of the front wheels.

He pulled one of the warm hot dogs out of the sack. "Come here, girl," he said, not knowing why he'd decided it was female. The dog's nose sniffed the sharp aroma. She licked her mouth and whimpered, but refused to come out. "Come on, now. I know you're hungry." He held the food closer. The dog cautiously bit a small piece off and swallowed it whole. Then she bit off a large chunk and wolfed it down. "That's a good girl." He reached out to pet her, but she shrank back. "You don't have to be afraid of me," he said in a patient, soothing voice. "I'm not going to hurt you."

He held the sack close to the dog's nose, hoping the enticing aroma of the hot dog and her intense hunger would draw her out. Before long, he managed to coax her out from under the truck. He let her sniff the bag then slowly started walking toward a side door. To his dismay, the dog wouldn't follow him. He broke off a piece of the last hot dog and held it to her nose. When she tried to grab it, he took a step backward toward the door. Little by little, he lured the dog toward the building. When he reached the door, he pulled out his key card then fed the dog the rest of the food. He used her preoccupation with the food to distract her long enough to sweep her into his arms. The dog yelped and struggled to get free, but didn't try to bite. He quickly swiped the card in the door lock and pulled on the handle with two fingers. Once inside, he set the dog on the carpet.

She collapsed and began to whimper again. Ryan didn't know what to do. He grew alarmed at her panting. "What's the matter, girl? Did the hot dog make you sick?"

Her docked tail managed to thump in response to his voice. She stared up at him with those big, sad eyes.

When she refused to move, he picked her up again and carried her to his room on the first floor walking as fast has his legs could carry him. Once in his room, he set her on the carpeting, got down on one knee and examined her. Something didn't look right. For a homeless dog, she sure had a round stomach...

He froze with alarm as the truth dawned on him. It was a *she* all right and *she* had a belly full of puppies.

Chapter Four

The hostess at the Sunnyside Café flashed a practiced smile. "Would you like a table for one or are you waiting for someone?"

"No," Katie replied. "I'm alone."

The hostess led her to a small table in the opposite corner. She sat down and opened her menu.

A balding, middle-aged waiter approached her. "Hi, my name is Carl and I'll be taking care of you tonight. Would you care to start with a beverage?"

She set down her menu. "I'd like a diet soda, please. What are your specials today?"

Carl looked up from his order pad. "We have a hot beef or a hot turkey sandwich with mashed potatoes and gravy and a vegetable for eight ninety-five."

"Does it take long to make?"

He shook his head. "I'll have it on the table in

five minutes."

She closed her menu. "I'd like the special with turkey, please."

After Carl left, she pulled out her phone to check her work email, but the conversation at the table behind her drew her attention instead. A young mother with dark hair swept back into a low ponytail sat with her two children—a four-year-old boy and a baby girl that Katie estimated to be around ten months old. The little boy wanted a pizza, but the mother told him he couldn't have it and he began to cry.

"No pizza tonight, Logan," Katie heard the mother say in a hushed, but worried voice. "We have to get something cheaper or I won't be able to buy your breakfast tomorrow."

The woman dug into a diaper bag, grumbling softly to herself as she pulled out a small jar of baby food. "If we're stuck here longer than that, I don't know what I'm going to do. This place is expensive." She stopped rummaging and placed one hand on her forehead, exhaling a tired sigh. "I'm going to run out of diapers, too."

The little boy didn't understand and continued

to cry. The mother tried to calm him, but he kept saying his stomach hurt.

"Honey, I know you're hungry," she whispered with a note of sadness in her voice. "We're going to get something to eat as soon as we can. Now don't cry. Here," she pushed a glass toward him, "drink some water."

Carl dropped off Katie's soda and moved on to the mother's table. Katie had stopped scrolling but kept her head down, listening intently.

"Did you mention you have a special today?"

Carl described the item and told the woman the price.

"I'll take a half-order of the special with beef for Logan. I need a glass of milk for the baby's bottle. Logan and I will just have water to drink."

"What would you like to order, Ma'am?"

She shook her head. "Nothing...thanks. I'm not hungry."

The pseudo cheerfulness in her voice, however, gave Katie a different impression.

Carl left and Logan began to fuss again. The sound of his crying broke Katie's heart and caused her to wonder how many children in the world were going to bed hungry tonight. She'd never experienced such a thing and hoped her future children never would, either.

Carl returned and set Katie's dinner in front of her. "Will there be anything else?"

She motioned to him to draw close. "Order a small cheese pizza for the little boy at the next table and make that hot beef special a full order for the mother," she whispered in his ear. "In the meantime, give him a cup of chicken noodle soup and a glass of juice to keep him busy while he waits. Put everything for them, including a piece of pie and a child's ice cream for dessert, on my bill."

He gave her a look of astonishment. "Who shall I say covered her tab?"

She waved the notion away. "I'm just paying it forward."

He thanked her and left, smiling.

Katie ate her dinner and went to the cashier to pay, passing a food runner from the kitchen bringing out the pizza for Logan and the hot beef sandwich for his mother. Carl met her at the cash register with the bill.

"That was nice of you to pick up the tab for that family," he said as he handed her the guest check.

Katie pulled her wallet out of her purse and handed the cashier a credit card. "It was no big deal. Just helping out a fellow traveler."

He placed his hand on her shoulder. "Maybe not to you, but to her it was a huge blessing. The young lady told me she's on her way to St. Paul to live with her sister. She's hoping to find a job there, but right now, her situation is pretty desperate. Everything she owns is packed into her car. Poor girl. I hope things get better for her."

"Yeah, me, too," Katie said soberly. She handed him a generous tip and went up to her suite.

By nine o'clock, she had showered, changed into her pajamas and retired for the night. She lay on her huge bed, tossing and turning, unable to sleep. Thoughts of Josh plagued her mind and the life they could have had if he'd survived. After an hour of struggling to quiet her mind, she sat up and turned on the light.

"Forget trying to fall asleep," she told herself. "You won't get a wink until you leave this room and all of the bad memories behind."

She threw back the covers and dragged herself out of bed. Her body ached, sluggish and weighed down from a stressful day, but her heart had lightened considerably.

Ten minutes later, Katie walked into the softly lit lobby dragging her suitcase behind. She stopped, disconcerted by the sight of wall-to-wall people attempting to sleep on mats on the floor. Once she surrendered her key to a registration clerk, she'd be somewhere in that crowd trying to do the same thing.

Across the room, a dark-haired woman in denim leggings and a faded sweatshirt sat on an ottoman, struggling to calm her fussing baby. The child's crying grew louder as the young woman tried to rock her to sleep. The people around her were stirring on their mats and grumbling about the noise. Katie recognized the young woman from the restaurant and her somber mood dropped even lower. Between the tight, makeshift accommodations and the clamor coming from the raucous crowd in the bar upstairs, both mother and child were in for a rough night.

She suddenly formed an idea. Deserting her suitcase for the moment, she maneuvered her way between bodies until she reached the woman. "Hi," Katie said in a hushed tone, "do you remember me?"

The young woman's eyes widened. "You're the person who paid for our dinner," she whispered back as a lock of dark, curly hair fell across her forehead. "Why did you leave so quickly? You didn't give me a chance to thank you."

"I didn't want any fanfare," Katie whispered in her ear. "I just wanted you and the kids to have a nice meal." She pulled her room key, still in its paper folder, from her jean pocket and held it out. "This is the key to my suite. It's yours for the next two nights if you choose to stay that long." She pressed the palm-sized folder into the woman's hand. "You'll find the room number written on the inside. The king suite comes with concierge services so you'll get a full breakfast in the clubroom and other snacks during the day. You and the kids enjoy the luxury. It's paid for in full."

The young woman stood up, staring at Katie with a look of incredulity. "You're giving me your suite? Why?"

Katie knew their voices were disturbing people. She leaned close. "I want the kids to have a decent place to stay until the storm is over."

The woman looked uncomfortable and tried to give the key back. "I can't take this. I have no way to pay you."

Katie pushed the key away. "I'm not asking for money. I simply want you to take it off my hands." The baby started fussing again. "You'd better get a move on. Your little one sounds pretty tired." She turned to go, but thought of something and whirled back again. "Oh, and if you need a diaper—or ten diapers—just call the front desk and ask them to send some up. The room comes with perks like that." The shocked, but grateful expression in the woman's tear-filled eyes made her day. "Have a good night." She turned all the way around this time and began to walk away.

"My name is Maggie," the woman called after her, sounding stunned but happy. "The kids are Logan and Ella. Thank you so much!"

A collective "Sh-h-h-h-h-h!" filled the air.

Katie waved goodbye and walked out of the room. She had no bed, no private bathroom and no prospects for a decent night's sleep but she hadn't felt this energized in a long time.

~*~

Ryan once again eased himself onto the bar stool and looked around the noisy room, searching for his friendly bartender. He didn't see Red anywhere and worried the man's shift had ended. This time, he actually needed to talk to the guy and get his advice. Red couldn't leave the resort, so where did he go?

He pulled out his phone to search the Internet for information on pregnant dogs.

"Hey, there," Red's voice boomed. "Back for another Killian's Amber?" He stood behind the bar, his beefy arms holding two cases of Budweiser. "The bar boy couldn't make it in today," he said and set the cases on the floor. "I'm doing double-duty tonight."

"No thanks." Ryan set his phone down and pulled out a couple bills. "I'll just have a Coke."

Red filled a tall glass with ice and picked up

the soda gun, filling the glass with bubbly cola. "Got problems?"

"How'd you know?"

Red chuckled. "After you've been in this business for a while, you learn to read faces." He set the soda in front of Ryan, along with a bowl of snack mix. "What's the matter?"

"I, ah..." Ryan cleared his throat. "Well, I...I found this dog outside by the entrance. She was curled up on a rug behind the planter." He toyed with the straw in his glass. "Anyway, I, ah...I felt sorry for her and brought her to my room to warm her up." He glanced up and met Red's curious gaze. "I'm no expert, but she looks like she's going to have puppies."

Red pulled his security card out of his pocket and swiped the cash register. "Oh, you mean Sadie?" He looked relieved as he keyed in his security code to unlock the cash drawer.

"*Who?*"

"Sadie." Red shoved the card back in his pocket. He paused, his gaze furtively scanning the area, as if to make sure no one else overheard him.

"Does the dog happen to be a black Cocker Spaniel with sad eyes?"

Amazed, Ryan sat up straight, focusing his full attention on Red's question. "Yeah, that's the one. How'd you know her name?"

"Everybody on staff knows Sadie. She's been hanging around since Thanksgiving weekend. The housekeeping crew and some of the girls on the kitchen staff named her. Everyone puts food out for her, but no one has been able to get close to her, much less catch her. How did you get her into your room?"

"I fed her a couple hot dogs."

Red burst out laughing. "Don't tell that to the girls in housekeeping. They've been trying to catch her with better food than that."

"What is the staff feeding her? I mean, does she need special food for her condition?"

Red reached under the counter and pulled a plate from the bus pan containing a large T-bone with scraps of meat still on it. "Lots of steak. She's eatin' like a queen." He grabbed a Styrofoam takeout container and dumped the bone into it. "I've got more." He went to work filling the white box until he could barely close the top. He set it on the counter then leaned close. "This is between you and me, okay? My manager gave us strict orders not to supply Sadie with any more food." He added with a mischievous smirk, "The boss has called the pound several times to pick her up, but she mysteriously disappears just before the dog catchers arrive." He quickly sobered. "What she needs is a permanent home. Do you plan to keep her?"

"Keep her?" Ryan swallowed hard and splayed his hand on his chest, dismayed at the black dog hair all over his gray sweater. He'd trekked up here to forget about his family issues for one weekend and spend some quality time on his sled, not to complicate his life even more by adopting a stray, pregnant dog. "Absolutely not."

He didn't want a dog, had no time to spend with a dog and didn't know what to do with a dog about to have puppies. Still, the fact that she didn't have a permanent home at a time when she needed a loving owner tugged at his heart. Perhaps he could find someone to take her...

Red moved to the other end of the bar to fill a

drink order for the cocktail server on duty. He whispered a few words to the twenty-something woman and her face blossomed with a huge smile. She pulled out her phone and began texting.

Ryan drained his Coke and threw a couple dollars on top of his coins on the bar. "See you later, Red. Thanks!" He grabbed his takeout box filled with bones and slid off the barstool—slamming into a blonde woman wearing an ivory sweater and a long blue scarf loosely knotted around her neck. She stopped short, almost falling backward over the small suitcase she tugged behind her.

The Styrofoam box crashed to the floor as Ryan grasped Katie McGowan by the arms, pulling her upright to restore her balance before they both toppled over. She grabbed onto his shirt to steady herself and they stood face-to-face.

A sudden, unexpected surge of warmth spread through his arms and chest.

"Sorry about that," he said gently. "I didn't mean to tackle you." He released her and stood back, but couldn't shake the desire to embrace her again. The natural fit of his arms cradling her still lingered in his mind. It felt right to hold her close. He had a sudden, crazy urge to run his fingers through the silky strands of her long blonde hair, but the guarded look in her eyes warned him to keep his distance.

He knelt on the floor and began gathering the steak bones scattered under his chair. "What's with the suitcase and the winter gear? Are you checking out?"

The suggestion sounded ludicrous, but he didn't know what else to think.

"Of course not," she said, looking mildly amused, though an off-key note in her voice and flushed cheeks hinted something was amiss. "Where would I go?" She rolled her suitcase out of the way to give him more room then turned back to him. "I gave up my room."

"*You did what?*" He tossed the last T-bone into the box and stood up. "Why on earth did you do that?"

She lifted her chin. "Because there's a family stranded in this hotel that needs a room a lot worse than I do," she asserted, scraping a glob of steak sauce off her slimming jeans. "I turned it over to a woman with two small children."

He shook his head, trying to figure out what she'd just said. "You're not making sense." He set the battered box on the counter. "If you don't have a room, where are you going to sleep?"

She shrugged. "I'll probably find a spot in the lobby with everyone else who doesn't have one. I'm sure I can get a blanket and pillow from the housekeeping staff."

"No, you're not!" He and Red shouted in unison as Red approached them.

She stared at him and Red as though *they'd* lost their minds.

"It's not safe," Ryan argued and made a sweeping gesture with his hand. "Do you have any idea how many guys in this bar have had too much to drink because they don't have anything better to do? Do you realize most of them are watching your every move right now?"

"Oh, come on," Katie argued. "I understand your concern, but the lobby is a public place. Nothing is going to happen to me there."

"Trust me, he's right," Red boldly interjected. "We have great security here, but incidents still happen."

She folded her arms and glared at them. "Then I'll sleep in my car..."

"You can have my room," Ryan insisted. "It's a large corner room, poolside, two queen beds. Really nice." *You can even have the dog to keep you company...*

"That's ridiculous," Katie argued. "I'm not going to take your room. I gave up mine willingly and the last thing I want to do is displace someone else."

"Why don't you two share it?" Red stood behind the bar with his hands out, palms upward, like a preacher giving a sermon. "I mean, you're adults. You can work something out, right?"

"Wrong!" Katie smacked her hand on the counter. "I'm not going to share a room with a guy I barely know. Are you crazy?" She turned to Ryan. "No offense, but talk about unsafe. You could be an ax murder, for all I know."

A ball of heat under Ryan's collar raced up the back of his neck and toward his face in record speed. Women had called him an assortment of unflattering names in his life, especially ex-girlfriends, but he'd never had a woman brand him with that label!

His astonishment must have shown on his face because she immediately softened.

"Hey, I'm sorry," she said with a rueful smile. "I didn't mean to overreact; it's just that I wouldn't be comfortable sharing a room with a guy I didn't know."

He agreed with her one hundred percent and gave her high marks for being cautious. Just the same, as a matter of pride, he wanted the chance to prove himself now.

"Red!"

Everyone turned toward the passionate cry as a young woman rushed into the bar. "Where is she? Who found her?" The short redhead wore stubby pigtails, a black spandex dress with matching leggings and ankle boots.

Red frowned and put a thick finger to his lips at the mention of finding the dog. "Mandy, meet my friend, er..." He gestured toward Ryan.

"Ryan Scott."

"Right. Ryan, this is my cousin, Mandy Walsh.

She's a hostess in the café." He gave Ryan a "thumbs up" gesture. "He's your man."

Mandy brushed past Katie and threw her arms, laden with bracelets, around Ryan's neck. "Oh, my gosh! I'm so grateful you rescued her that I could just kiss you!"

Ryan gently loosened her grip on him and put some space between them. "That's quite all right." He chuckled, taken aback by her excitement. "No additional thanks needed."

"Where is she?" Red and green Christmas bells dangling from Mandy's ears jingled while she talked. "Is she okay? I want to see her!"

"No problem. She's in my room, resting," Ryan replied, wondering if the blessed event was happening this very minute. "Well, I hope that's *all* she's doing." He didn't know how to tell such things, but from the size of Sadie's stomach, it looked to him like it wouldn't be long.

Katie grabbed the handle of her suitcase and paused. "It sounds like you have plenty of excitement going on in your room already. I need to get going. Excuse me."

She tried to pass him, but Ryan stepped in her way. "Please, Katie, wait. It's not what you think. We can't talk about it here, but you're right—there is something going on in my room and I definitely want you to be a part of it."

She answered with a wry laugh. "I don't understand what you're getting at, but I'm *not* interested."

Mandy whirled around. "What's the matter with you? Don't you care about Sadie?" She moved in close, getting in Katie's face. "You'd better not rat on us or I'll—"

"Mandy!" Red's angry face puffed up like a tomato.

"Whoa, whoa..." Ryan said, getting in between them. "Let's start over, okay?" He turned to Katie. "Remember that sound you heard when we were walking into the hotel?" She didn't answer, but her gorgeous blue eyes widened with keen interest. "Yeah, you heard a whimper all right, but when we looked around, we missed the one spot where we would have found her."

Katie gasped. "Who did you find? She must have been freezing!"

Ryan moved in closer. "Sadie has a really thick coat." He glanced around to make sure no one in the noisy, crowded bar could overhear his conversation. "A little while ago, I walked outside and heard it again. Unfortunately, the bell captain found her first and kicked her off her mat behind the planter."

Mandy sucked in a deep breath. "He kicked her? Oh, no-o-o-o..."

Ryan turned to Mandy and placed his hand on her trembling shoulder, regretting he'd divulged that part. "Don't worry, she's okay." He handed her a cocktail napkin to wipe a large tear from her cheek. "It looked more like a push to me. As far as I can tell, she's fine—and in good hands now."

"I soooo love you for saving her..." Mandy said with a loud sob.

"Yeah, well..." Ryan cleared his throat and turned back to Katie. "She ran away and it bothered me so much to know she had no protection from the weather that I tracked her down. She ate the hot dogs I bought for her, but wouldn't follow me so I picked her up and carried her to my room. That's when I saw her condition."

Katie stared at Mandy, Red and Ryan with a

look of utter confusion. "What's wrong with...Sadie?"

Ryan sighed. "She's pregnant. *Very* pregnant, and due to drop her load any day now." He ran his hand through his hair. "I just hope nothing goes wrong. I don't know anything about delivering pups."

He stared up at the ceiling, hoping that dog had a guardian angel with veterinarian training because she needed one like yesterday.

"Sadie is a *dog*?" Katie responded to her own question with an incredulous laugh. "What breed?"

A black Cocker, Red silently mouthed.

"I can't wait to see her!" Mandy said and grabbed Katie's hand. "Will you come, too?"

"Of course," Katie said, softening her tone. "I'll help in any way I can."

Mandy wedged herself between Ryan and Katie and grabbed his hand, too, causing him to wonder if they were going to sing and dance as they followed the Yellow Brick Road to Emerald City. She looked up at him expectantly. "Can we go now?"

Nice going, Scott. Your quiet, stress-free weekend is turning into a three-ring circus.

Ryan pulled his hand away, weary of Mandy's fondness for touchy-feely drama. "Why don't you girls go on ahead? I need to get a new box for these bones, but I'll be right behind you. Here's my key. I'm in room 104."

He watched Mandy lead Katie out of the lounge pulling her suitcase and coat behind her, hoping he could somehow find a way to convince Katie to take his room before the night ended.

Chapter Five

Katie surveyed the busy pool area as she waited for Mandy to unlock the door to Ryan's room. Parents stretched out in lounge chairs or soaked in the hot tub, socializing while their children were tossing beach balls, running and jumping into the water, even though the rules on the wall specifically forbade it. Screams of laughter echoed off the cement walls. The odor of chlorine filled the warm, humid air.

Mandy opened the door and burst in. "Sadie! Sadie, where are you?"

Katie closed the door to block out the noise from the pool area, but didn't latch it so Ryan could enter without a key. The room held two queen-sized beds flanked by nightstands, a large dresser, a desk, a brass floor lamp and a loveseat. She made a cursory check of the open areas, but didn't see the dog.

Mandy found Sadie lying behind the loveseat.

"My poor baby! Are you okay?"

Katie set her suitcase to one side, kneeled on the loveseat and peered over the back. Sadie lay on the beige carpet with her back to the corner. The furry black mound looked up at her with a sorrowful expression in her large, round eyes. Katie's heart wrenched at the sight of her swollen tummy.

I'd be sad, too, if I found myself homeless in your condition.

Mandy began to pet the dog and speak soothing words. Sadie shrank back at first, but Mandy's steady, gentle touch eased the dog's fear. Sadie began to wag her short tail in response, but she didn't get up.

Katie reached down and stroked Sadie's thick, wavy fur. "She's such a sweet dog. I don't understand how anyone could desert her," Katie remarked when Sadie licked the back of her hand. "Does she belong to you?"

"Sadie belongs to all the people here who care about her." Mandy sat up, leaning her back against the wall and pulling her knees to her chest. "We noticed her sleeping in the walk-in trash bin every morning, eating scraps on the ground. We didn't know if someone lost her or deliberately left her behind, but her owner has never contacted the resort or the local animal shelter, so we've assumed the person abandoned her."

"Why didn't someone take her home and care for her?"

Mandy caressed one of Sadie's long, feathery ears. "We've tried to catch her, but she'd always run away." She rested her head against the wall. "I don't understand why she responded to Ryan and not us girls, but perhaps her former owner resembled him."

Katie's heart warmed at the thought of Ryan caring enough about a stray dog to go after her in a snowstorm and carry her in his arms to safety. "A guy who fed her hotdogs..."

Someone rapped lightly on the door.

Katie rose and headed across the room. "That must be Ryan." She slid open the door and instead encountered a young woman in a housekeeping uniform, her long brown hair woven into a single thick braid.

"Hi," the woman said shyly, "is Mandy here?"

"Come on in, Susan!"

Katie stood aside for Mandy's coworker to enter. Susan went straight for Sadie and knelt on the floor beside her. "Hello there little mamma," she whispered and gently held out the back of her hand for the dog to sniff. "How are you doing?"

"This is Susan," Mandy said to Katie, "my best friend since first grade." Mandy pushed the loveseat out of the way then moved over for Susan to sit next to the dog. "Katie is Ryan's girlfriend."

Katie's head snapped up. "I'm not his girlfriend. We're barely friends."

Mandy gave her a puzzled look. "Really? The way he looked at you in the lounge made me think you two were together."

The way he...what?

In a sudden burst of giddiness, Katie grabbed her purse and walked over to her suitcase. She pulled up the handle. "It has been nice meeting you both, but I'd better get going."

"What's the hurry? Mandy said. "You don't have anywhere to go, anyway."

"I need to get a few hours of sleep before the storm lets up. I plan to head home early in the morning."

The door opened while she was talking and Ryan walked in carrying the steak bones in a plastic bag. "How is the dog?"

As their gazes met, Mandy's words rang in her ears. *The way he looked at you in the lounge made me think you two were together.*

"Um..." Katie said, her mind going blank. Everyone stared at her, including the dog, waiting for her to get her brain in gear and finish the sentence. "...s-she's doing just fine."

Someone pounded on the door. Ryan opened it and another girl, tall and dark-haired, wearing a housekeeping uniform and carrying a large purse stood peering in. When she saw Mandy and Susan, she rushed past Ryan. "Mr. Jameson is coming this way. We've gotta hide." She spun around. "Hurry up, get in the bathroom!"

Mandy and Susan sprang off the floor.

"Move the loveseat!" Mandy cried. "We have to conceal the dog!"

In the fashion of a Chinese fire drill, the girls shoved the loveseat back into its original spot and ran into the bathroom, nearly knocking each other down in the process.

Within seconds, the manager appeared at the door. Ryan set the steak bones on the dresser and pulled the door all the way open. Echoes of laughter in the pool area, splashing water and the patter of small feet rapidly pounding on the pavement heralded the man's arrival.

"Sir, may I help you?" The words flowed naturally, as though Ryan used that level of politeness every day.

The tall, blond manager eyed Ryan suspiciously. "Someone reported seeing you carrying a dog into the building. Are you keeping an animal in this room?"

"No, sir," Ryan replied and stood aside. "I don't own a dog. Feel free to come in and look around if you'd like."

Mr. Jameson poked his head through the door and scanned the room. Katie stepped aside to allow him a better view. She treated him to an innocent smile, but behind her back, her fingers were tightly crossed. He gave her a hard stare. "Did he carry it into *your* room?"

Ryan moved to her side. "This *is* her room." He slid his arm around her waist and pulled her close, pressing her against the solid muscles of his broad chest. "We're staying here together."

Katie smiled again to play her part and attest they were *together*, but something in the way Ryan said those words made her pulse jump. It sounded so natural.

"Just so you know," the manager said in a warning tone, "animals aren't allowed in the hotel. People with pets must stay in the condo units and pay a damage deposit of one hundred dollars per animal. Do you understand the rules?"

Their heads nodded in unison, like toy bobblehead dolls.

"Very well," he said and turned to leave. "Enjoy your stay."

They stood in silence, watching the man walk away.

"That was a close call," Ryan said with a smile and gazed down at her. "We make a good team."

Before she could agree, the bathroom door opened a crack.

"Is he gone?"

Ryan laughed. "Yes, you can come out, now."

The girls burst out of the small room with loud sighs of relief.

Katie didn't realize Ryan still had his arm around her until Mandy saw them standing side-by-side. "I thought you said you weren't together."

"W-we're not," Katie said as they pulled apart.

Mandy replied with a sly grin. "Sure looked like it to me."

The dark-haired girl stepped forward. "Hi, I'm Nila. You don't mind if we hang out here for a while and keep watch over Sadie, do you? Mandy says Sadie might be getting close to having her babies and I'd really like to be with her when the puppies are born. Sadie is...well...special to us."

Ryan picked up the bag of steak bones and offered them to Nila. "Why don't you take her to your room? I'll even risk carrying her over there for you."

"We don't have a room," the girls said in an off-key chorus.

"The staff is bedding down in several of the

conference rooms," Susan added. "We don't have a place to keep her safely out of sight."

Mandy's phone beeped. She pulled it out and started texting a reply. "The snack bar is closing in fifteen minutes. I'm ordering a couple pizzas. What do you guys want on them?"

Susan and Nila began to argue over what kind of pizza to order, but their conversation came to an abrupt halt when Sadie began to whine.

Everyone rushed to the loveseat and crowded around it to check on the dog. Sadie lay on her side, panting.

"Do you think she's in labor?" Katie asked. No one answered her and it occurred to her everyone feared the same thing. What would they do if the dog had complications giving birth? She decided to stick around a little longer—for Sadie's sake. She didn't know anything about delivering puppies, but she knew she wouldn't be able to sleep now with the dog's predicament on her mind. "I don't know much about pregnant dogs, but I don't think she should be going anywhere."

Everyone stared at Ryan.

"Okay, okay," he said resignedly and threw his hands in the air. "Do whatever you think is best. Just don't let her die giving birth in my room."

"Really, Ryan." Mandy rolled her eyes. "You're so dramatic."

~*~

Ryan stared down at Sadie in dismay. She'd refused to chew on the steak bones they set out for her and had begun to pace in her corner. He figured having such a heavy belly caused her discomfort, but her loss of appetite worried him. He wondered what they could do to make her more comfortable. "Shouldn't she be in a box or something?"

"Yeah, it's called a whelping box," Nila said as she sat cross-legged on one of the beds scrolling on her iPhone. "Sadie needs one to keep her puppies warm." She stopped reading and looked up. "I just found a great web site on Cocker Spaniels. It has a how-to section with videos and everything on delivering a litter of puppies."

"That's a great idea," Katie said, walking toward her suitcase. She unzipped the lower front pocket and pulled out her laptop. "I just hope the storm hasn't affected our Internet service." She curled up on the loveseat and opened the cover.

Ryan sat next to her and watched her bring up Lakewood's Wi-Fi connection page. "Click on that green box," he said, moving closer to get a better look at the screen. "You don't have a room number, so put mine in instead."

"What number is it again?" Katie said, moving her fingers over the touchpad.

Without thinking, Ryan slid his arm across the back of the loveseat and angled his head to get a better view of the information. "It's one zero..." The light scent of her floral perfume filled his nostrils. He sat still for a moment, confused.

What was I going to say?

"Is that all? I thought your room had three numbers," Katie asked.

"Ah...yeah, it's one zero four," he said, getting back to business. "Click on that red box and you should get connected to Lakewood's home page."

"Gosh, this is going slow." Katie sighed with impatience. "I need a new computer."

Ryan moved closer to examine the problem. "I doubt it's the laptop. There are probably a lot of people in the hotel right now using the Wi-Fi."

Susan stood up. "I saw some boxes piled up this morning inside the back door and a couple of them were quite large. I'll walk over to the kitchen and see if they're still there."

Nila climbed off the bed and tossed her phone on the pillow. "I'll go raid the housekeeping room for a blanket or some old towels." She followed Susan to the door. "If the pizzas get here before we get back, save some for us!"

Nila and Susan opened the door and paused. "Mandy," Susan said peering over her shoulder, "did you order soda with the pizzas?" She stared at Mandy—hard—as if communicating a silent message. "We can't have pizza without Coke."

"Huh?" Mandy looked confused. "Oops, I forgot. I'm sorry! It's too late to get it from the snack bar and the vending machines are a major rip off." She chewed on the side of her lip as her gaze shifted from her friends to Ryan and Katie sitting together on the sofa. She stood up and grabbed her purse. "Okay, I'll go to the lounge and get a pitcher of diet Coke from Red."

The girls trooped out of the room and closed

the door. The room suddenly seemed too quiet.

Katie looked up from her computer. "Is it just me, or did they order pizza for us then take off on purpose to leave us here together?"

It didn't take a genius to recognize the girls were matchmaking, but Ryan decided not to make a big deal of it. He didn't want Katie to feel uncomfortable and leave. "They'll be back." He pointed to the screen and changed the subject. "You need to start over."

Katie groaned at the "connection timed-out" message and closed her laptop.

"Try again in an hour," Ryan said with a wry grin, "after the baby boomers call it a night. Most of them are either shopping online right now, looking for last minute deals or lurking on Facebook."

"You're probably right." She smiled at his explanation, but her amusement quickly turned to worry. "I just hope Sadie holds out for another hour."

Someone rapped on the door.

"That must be the pizzas." Ryan sprang off the loveseat and dug into his pocket for a couple bills as he crossed the room and opened the door. He signed the receipt to charge the food to his room and handed the guy a tip. Using the side of his foot, he shut the door again and placed the large, flat boxes on the desk along with napkins and paper plates.

"It smells *good*," Katie remarked and peeked into the top box. "This one is sausage." She flipped open the lid. "I ate dinner, but I'm suddenly starving." Pulling out two pieces, she placed them on a paper plates and handed one to Ryan. His mouth watered at the pungent aroma filling the room.

They went back to the loveseat and sat down.

"So, where are you from?" Katie asked with a mouthful of pizza.

"I've got a place in Edina," Ryan replied. "I bought a house a couple years ago. How about you? I recall your mentioning once about going home to Minneapolis."

Katie set her pizza back on her plate. "I have an apartment in Golden Valley, but my parents live in Minneapolis proper in the Bryn Mawr neighborhood. That's where I grew up." She licked her fingers. "What brings you to Lakewood for Christmas? Is your family staying here as well?"

"No," Ryan said, his chest tightening at the mention of his family. "My parents cancelled Christmas this year and filed for divorce instead. Dad's celebrating his independence in Hawaii with his thirty-five-year-old girlfriend and Mom went to Paris on a power-shopping trip." He took another bite of pizza, but it didn't taste nearly as good as it had a moment ago.

"Gosh, I'm sorry to hear that." Katie stared at him wide-eyed. "What about the rest of your family? Don't you want to get together with them on Christmas?"

Ryan waved his hand, communicating an emphatic *no* before she finished speaking. "I turned my sister down. Don't get me wrong, she has a great husband and kids but she's more upset than I am about the uncertainty of our family business. If the Mercedes dealership becomes a casualty of the divorce, we may both lose our jobs. I want to support her in any way I can, but what I *don't* want is to spend my holiday rehashing a crisis that's beyond our control."

"That sounds like a cop-out to me." Katie met his gaze with a skeptical look. "Aren't you treating your sister the same way your parents are treating you?"

"I'm doing us both a favor," he argued. "We need to accept the impact of the divorce, whatever it may be, and adjust." He wiped his fingers on a napkin and set his plate aside. How did a perfectly normal conversation suddenly take such a wrong turn? "We can't control what other people do, Katie. We can only accept it and move on." He let out a cynical laugh. "I came up here to take a break from the drama and yet, here I am, discussing my personal problems with you."

"Obviously, you *do* need to talk about it." She set her plate aside and leaned toward him, confronting him. "Are you sure you came up here to get a break, or are you simply turning your back on Christmas to hide out and lick your wounds?"

He matched her stare for stare. "Lady, I'm not hiding from anything. I live for the days when I'm barreling across the lake at full throttle and tearing up fresh powder with my sled." He saw her recoil, but the words came out before he could stop himself. "You ought to try it sometime. It'll give you some great memories."

Her eyes widened with shock, her face paling as the words sunk in. She swallowed hard.

He watched her sudden transformation and blinked in astonishment. What just happened?

"Katie, what's wrong? What did I say?"

She bolted off the loveseat and stood in the center of the room. "You have no idea how much those words hurt," she spat, turning away with her hands clenched.

He rose from the loveseat and stood behind her. With a gentle touch, he placed his hand on her arm. "I'm sorry. I-I didn't mean to upset you."

"It doesn't matter. You didn't know what you were saying." She pulled away as tears pooled in her eyes. "I have to leave."

Panic filled his heart. Ryan didn't understand what had set her off, but he desperately needed to find out. He didn't want their friendship to end this way. "Please...stay." He moved closer and spoke into her ear. "Whatever is bothering you won't go away until you talk it through with someone." Placing his hand on her arm once more, he waited briefly to see if she would allow it then slowly turned her around. "Talk to me, Katie. Tell me why I made you cry. I promise I'll never do it again."

She glared at him, tears streaming down her face. "What is it about men and their reckless disregard for human life? Why do you have to risk everything for a few minutes of worthless thrill?"

His mouth fell open. Reckless disregard for human life? A few minutes of worthless thrill? "Tell me what happened," he said, coming to the realization she'd been through something so terrible it had scarred her forever. "I'm a good listener."

She walked over to the loveseat and glanced behind it to check on the dog. It seemed as though she'd changed her mind, but he knew her action stemmed from simply needing something to do to stave off the nervous energy generated from opening an old wound. "It happened here at Lakewood about two years ago." She looked up. "Josh and I had only been married for ten days. We'd just finished a seven-day cruise in the Caribbean and since we still had some vacation time left, we decided to run up to Lakewood for a couple days of sledding to round out our honeymoon."

He suddenly knew where this story was going

and understood what he'd said that caused her reaction. But understanding didn't make it right or lessen his regret. He stood silently, waiting for her to continue.

"We rented the honeymoon suite," Katie said and picked her discarded paper plate off the carpet. "It looked similar to the one the hotel gave me to stay in tonight. Now you know why I couldn't stay there." She folded the plate in half and tossed it into the trashcan under the desk. "The woman I gave my suite to needed it a lot worse than I did so my decision to leave it worked out for the best."

"Your reaction this afternoon in the lobby gave me quite a start," Ryan added. "You looked like you'd seen a ghost, literally. I knew you had a problem, but at the time, you acted like you were okay so I figured I didn't have any business asking."

"It didn't matter." She gave him a rueful smile. "I wouldn't have told you the truth, anyway." She walked over to her suitcase and picked up her purse. "We hung around the hotel on our first day. I had jetlag and still felt the swaying of the ship every time I stood up, so I couldn't muster the energy to jump on a sled right away. The next day, we headed out early. It had snowed during the night and we were delighted to have a few inches of fresh powder to play with."

"So you used to drive a sled?"

"Yes, we had matching Polaris." She opened her purse and began rummaging around in it. "They were red, our favorite color."

"Ever been on one since that time?"

Her eyes narrowed. "Not on your life." She paused, wincing at the bad pun then pulled out a small photograph. "This is my husband, Josh."

Ryan took the photo and perused the congenial face of a man in his middle thirties with short brown hair and greenish-gray eyes. The image looked familiar. Then it all came back. He'd heard talk about the accident in his circle of friends, but he also remembered seeing it on the news. He handed the snapshot back to her.

Katie shoved the photo back into her purse then pulled out a tissue and blotted her streaked face. "We found a group going out so we joined them. We'd only made it about a mile when we came to an area where the trails crossed and we pulled up to the four-way stop to wait for everyone to catch up before we took off again. We should have kept going—" Her voice broke as her eyes pooled with fresh tears.

Ryan rushed to her side and wrapped his arms around her. "Take it easy, Katie. You don't have to finish if it's too painful. I don't need to know the rest."

"No," Katie said and pressed her palms against his chest. "I want you to know what happened. I need you to understand what I'm going through." She didn't push him away, but continued to use her hands as a buffer. "We heard another group of sleds approaching from the opposite way. I didn't know it at the time, but the men had been drinking all night. I could tell they were driving much too fast. One guy didn't see the stop sign until too late. Truthfully, I don't know if he saw it at all because he came straight toward me. Josh jumped off his sled and pushed me out of the way, but before he could clear out, the other sled hit mine head on. The impact flipped the sled upside down and pinned Josh underneath." She began to sob. "...he died instantly."

Ryan tightened his hold on her, resting his cheek on the top of her head. He stayed quiet, simply holding her in his arms until her grief subsided.

"You're a strong woman," he said at last. "I don't know many people who could survive such a crisis and keep their sanity intact."

She gazed up at him. "This hotel is full of people, but I've never known so much loneliness in my life. It's not because I've ended up back at the place where it all happened, though. No matter what I do, whether I'm traveling for work or spending time at my parents' home, I can't seem to fill the hollow spot inside me."

Ryan gazed into her misty blue eyes and saw a lonely, broken soul. Like him.

His pulse began to race. He'd only known Katie for one day, but long enough to realize he wanted to see more of her—a lot more. This snowstorm had an end date, but their friendship could last forever. He hoped it would someday grow into something more. At this point, he had no clue how to define *more*, but he didn't care. For now, just being with Katie and taking things one day at a time would be enough.

"You're not alone, Katie. Not anymore," he said, taking a chance that she'd listen to reason. "I'm here for you."

The door burst open and Bippity, Boppity and Boo entered, their jaws collectively dropping at the sight of Ryan with his arms around Katie. Instead of pulling apart, Ryan kept his arms around her as the girls filed into the room, staring at him and Katie with great interest.

Something had changed between them. Now everyone knew it.

Chapter Six

At 11 p.m., Katie sat curled up on the loveseat with her laptop, researching Cocker Spaniels, the stages of canine labor and tips on whelping a litter of puppies. Ryan's advice about waiting an hour to try connecting again to the Wi-Fi rang true. All of the baby boomers staying in the hotel must have signed off and gone to bed. Her computer connected quickly and easily.

"Do you want any more pizza, Katie?" Nila held up the box that had contained the one with sausage. The bottom of it had a large stain that looked like one huge grease spot. "There's one piece left."

"No thanks," Katie said, cringing inwardly at the thought of eating cold, congealed pizza. Some people raved about it, but to her it looked gross. "I'm pretty full."

"Anyone else want pizza?" Nila scanned the room for any other takers. "Going, going..." She grinned. "Breakfast for me."

Ryan sat next to Katie on the loveseat, watching a movie on TV, but keeping the sound at a low hum. Sadie had settled down measurably in the last hour, despite numerous trips outside to piddle, and they wanted her to stay that way.

According to Katie's research, Sadie needed a quiet, stress-free environment. Sadie had taken up residence behind the loveseat and no one could get her to come out except for piddle breaks, so they'd given up trying to get her to bed down in the closet and put her makeshift whelping box in the spot of *her* choosing.

Mandy and Susan stretched out on one of the beds, watching the movie with Ryan while Nila sat cross-legged on the other bed, scrolling on her iPad. She'd changed out of her housekeeping uniform into black velour leggings and a hip-length sweater in gold. She had "baby-watch" for the next hour, which meant checking on the dog every fifteen minutes and taking her outside to do her business.

Nila slid off the bed and padded barefoot toward Sadie's corner. "Do you think this box will be big enough for her and the pups when they come?"

Katie stood up and stretched. She'd been sitting on that loveseat for an hour. She peered behind the small sofa and observed Sadie in her new digs—a large, low-sided cardboard box. Sadie lay on an old, faded blanket that Nila had borrowed from the housekeeping room. She looked tired and very uncomfortable.

"It will have to do," Katie said and sat down again next to Ryan. "Poor Sadie. She looks miserable. I hope her pups come tonight. I'd hate to leave tomorrow with her still in this condition."

She twisted in her seat and looked down at the dog. Sadie stared up at her with sad eyes, as though begging her to stay.

~*~

Early the next morning, Katie awoke in a dim room to find herself sitting on the loveseat with Ryan's arm around her shoulders, her face buried in his chest. Disoriented, she sat up and looked around groggily, wondering about the time. The mouthwatering aroma of fresh coffee and grilled bacon filled her nostrils, making her hungry.

Mandy and Nila slept peacefully on the beds, still in their clothes. Someone had tossed blankets over them and turned off the lights as well as the TV. Susan sat next to Mandy, dressed in a fresh housekeeping uniform, eating her breakfast from a white Styrofoam container. Her long brown braid, still damp from showering, fell over one shoulder.

Katie yawned. "What time is it?"

"It's almost seven," Susan said quietly and forked a fluffy chunk of scrambled eggs into her mouth. "I'm on duty in ten minutes, but I came back to rouse the girls. They both have to be to work in an hour." She picked up a large Styrofoam cup of coffee and blew on the liquid then cautiously brought it to her lips for a sip.

Ryan awoke and stretched out his long arms as a huge yawn overtook him. The dark shadow of his day-old beard gave him a woodsy, rugged look. He smiled at Katie as he gently brushed a lock of hair from her face. "Mornin'."

"Hey, there," Katie whispered, remembering the warmth of his firm chest, the musky fragrance lingering on his shirt. "We must have fallen asleep watching TV."

A dark smudge on his chest caught her eye. "Sorry about that," she said and pointed toward a spot where her mascara had rubbed off on his shirt.

He simply smiled, but the sparkle in his eyes told her it was worth it.

"Everyone fell asleep," Susan said and laughed. "It must have been a pretty boring movie! I woke up in the middle of the night and turned everything off."

Katie licked her lips, yearning for a cup of coffee. Her mouth tasted like garlic and sausage from last night's pizza. Her back ached from sitting in the same position all night. "Did you check on Sadie?"

Susan nodded grimly. "Twice; no dice. She's still in limbo." She bit into a crisp piece of bacon. "I took her outside as soon as I got up. Don't worry; it was so early no one saw us."

"How is the weather?"

"Can't tell if it's still snowing or just blowing around," Susan said and picked up a triangular piece of buttered toast. "The wind was so bad I couldn't go outside with Sadie. She did her thing while I watched from the door." She shivered and took another sip of coffee. "I saw the weather report on the TV in the café while I waited for my food. The blizzard isn't over yet. In fact, it's gotten worse."

"What?" Katie suddenly became fully awake. She sprang off the loveseat. "When is it going to end?"

Susan shrugged. "I don't know." She looked downcast. "I guess we're stuck here another day, though."

"What did you say?" Mandy said sleepily. She rolled over and blinked hard, trying to focus as she stared up at Susan. "We're stuck here again—on Christmas Eve?"

Nila raised her head, groaned then buried her face back in the pillow. "I want to go home!"

Ryan rose from the loveseat and took Katie by the hand. "Come on, Sunshine, I'll buy you breakfast so these girls can shower and get ready for work. We'll watch the weather report in the café." He waved at the girls as he pulled Katie out the door.

"I hate to think of all the travelers stuck in this hotel missing Christmas Eve with their families—

especially the children," Katie remarked, the disbelief in her voice echoing off the concrete walls of the pool area. "I have to see the weather report before I'll believe it!"

In the café, the hostess seated them at the last available booth. Ryan ordered coffee for two while they studied the menu. A hush fell over the crowd as a "breaking news" report appeared on the televisions mounted in each corner of the room. Cancellation notices of Christmas Eve church services crawled continuously across the bottom of the screen.

Katie watched with a sinking heart at the weatherman's map showing a huge white oval in west central Minnesota, representing the scope and path of the blizzard. The wind speeds were reportedly thirty to fifty miles per hour, gusting up to sixty miles per hour. A loud chorus of groans followed the announcement of "no travel" for the next twelve to twenty-four hours.

Their server brought two steaming mugs of coffee and took their order. They sat for a long time in bored silence, drinking their coffee and watching the news. Katie stared at the TV and doodled on her paper placemat, wondering how to fill the empty hours stretching ahead of her.

They were finished eating breakfast and drinking their last cup of coffee when Mandy came on duty at the hostess stand. She waved and walked over to their table wearing her leggings, ankle boots and a long black T-shirt shirt under a green blazer with "Lakewood Resort and Conference Center" embroidered on the pocket.

"We might as well get going," Katie said as she grabbed her purse and slid out of the booth. "I see you have a lot of people waiting for tables." Mandy was in for a busy morning, but at least she had something to do.

Mandy tossed a bar towel on the table and swiftly gathered up the cups and water glasses, placing them on a tray. "We had a staff meeting before I came on duty and Mr. Jameson announced he's planning a Christmas Eve celebration." She placed the tray on a chair and busily wiped down the table. "The idea started out as a party for the kids but once my coworkers became involved, it quickly turned into an all-day event for everyone." She paused, beaming with anticipation. "The concierge is in charge of the organizing committee and because we're already operating with a limited staff, she's looking for volunteers. Susan, Nila and I plan to sign up to help after our shifts. Why don't you join us?"

"All right," Katie said, intrigued. "I'd like that."

At the cashier, Katie scanned the restaurant, taking note of the children eating breakfast with their parents while she waited for Ryan to pay the bill. There were many kids in the hotel and each one deserved to have as much fun on Christmas Eve as she'd had growing up—regardless of the circumstances. To make the event a success, everyone needed to get involved.

"Thanks for breakfast, Ryan," Katie said as they left the café and entered the noisy lobby. People were busy piling their mats and bedding on an empty housekeeping cart. A small group of children played tag, laughing as they chased each other around the huge room. "I'm going back to the room to shower and change. I'll check on the dog, too. What are your plans for today?"

Ryan rubbed the dark growth on his jaw. "Same thing, but I'll wait my turn. I'm going to the bar to find out what time the pre-game show starts for the NFL game this afternoon." He took her hand in his. "Meet me for lunch?"

"Okay." She waved goodbye and headed toward the pool area. "The room is yours in an hour."

A housekeeping cart blocked the door of Ryan's room. Katie entered and found Susan making the beds. Sadie waddled behind her.

"Hi, Susan!"

Katie went straight to the dog and petted her. "Hello, there, little girl. How are you doing?" Sadie wagged her stubby tail. "She seems better today."

Susan piled pillows on one of the beds and pulled the bedspread over them. "I took her outside to potty a little while ago so she's good for now. The pool is closed this morning for maintenance so we don't have to worry about sneaking her out. She has fresh water and a meaty steak bone to chew on, but she doesn't seem very hungry." Susan gathered a pile of sheets in her arms. "I'm done here, so I have to get going. Have you signed up to help with the party?"

"I'm going to see the concierge right after I

take my shower."

"Okay," Susan replied with a smile. "I'll meet up with you after my shift."

Katie stood at the door and watched Susan push her cart to the next room, noting the girl's cheerfulness. Besides missing Christmas Eve with her family, she had to work. Instead of feeling sorry for herself, however, she'd chosen to focus on others.

An hour later, Karen Carpenter's smooth voice crooned "I'll Be Home For Christmas" through the lobby as Katie stood by the concierge desk, reviewing the volunteer opportunities for the day's itinerary posted on the wall. She'd signed up for several events, including the children's gift list, where she chose to sponsor Logan and Ella. After that, she went to the gift shop to purchase Christmas presents for them. To her dismay, many of the shelves in the children's section looked bare.

A young woman with shoulder-length black hair wearing a light blue dress stood behind the counter. "Good morning, may I help you?" The little shop smelled of pine bows and cinnamon.

"I hope so," Katie said, walking toward her. "I

need to buy something for a baby girl and a boy of about four years old.

The woman helped her select a large stuffed animal for Ella, two wooden puzzles and a coloring book with washable colored markers for Logan. While the woman wrapped her gifts, Katie passed the time browsing and came upon a red collar and matching leash with "Lakewood Resort" printed on them in a bin of discontinued items.

"I'll take these, too," she said and placed the pet items on the counter. She paid for her purchases and was on her way out the door when a decorative wooden crate filled with handmade ski caps caught her eye. One of the knitted caps looked the same gray color as the sweater Ryan had worn yesterday, with blue edging. She picked up the cap and went back to the cashier. "I'd like to buy this, and yes, please wrap it."

She took her presents for Maggie's children and placed them on the growing collection of gifts under the Christmas tree.

Her phone began blaring music in her purse. She knew the caller by the ring tone. "Hi, Mom!"

"Katie, your father and I are watching the news

and we've heard some areas are without power," her mother's crackly voice echoed over the line. "We're worried about you. Is everything okay where you're staying?"

"Yes, Mom," Katie said as she rearranged her gifts under the tree. "Everything seems to be working fine here. So far, so good, anyway."

"Still, I'm worried about your having to stay at the Lakewood...given the circumstances. How are you getting along?"

"I'm fine, Mom." She stood up and spotted a couple youngsters racing toward her. One of the little boys tripped and almost crashed into the tree. She smiled and helped him to his feet, but wagged her finger at him as he took off again. "I'm...I'm dealing with it."

"Are you sure?"

Katie glanced around the beautiful, festive room, taking in the huge decorated tree and the crackling fire. The pungent aromas of pine, spiced cider and freshly baked gingerbread cookies filled the air. "Yes, Mom, I'm sure. Don't worry about me."

Her mother sighed. "I can't help it. You're all alone...in that place...on Christmas Eve. I hope it isn't making you depressed."

But I'm not alone. I'm in a hotel filled with joyful people and many are worse off than I am.

Her elated mood began to deflate like a punctured tire at the whine in her mother's voice. "I have to go, Mom. The connection is going bad. It must be from the storm. I can barely hear you."

"You call me tonight when the family is here so we can all wish you a Merry Christmas."

Katie stared at the ceiling, surprised for wanting to end this conversation. She'd always welcomed her mother's concern in the past, especially during the holidays, but receiving the third degree, albeit well intentioned, suddenly made her restless. "I will, Mom. Yes, I'll call you later. I promise."

"All right then. Goodbye."

"Goodbye, Mom."

Katie turned off the phone and tossed it back into her purse. She needed to show up for her first volunteer assignment in ten minutes. Her heart thrummed with anticipation. She had a new mission—at least, for today—and new energy to fuel her purpose. She couldn't wait to get started.

~*~

Ryan sat on the loveseat, putting on his socks and tennis shoes. It felt good to shower and shave off the day-old growth on his jaw. He'd changed into a red flannel shirt and black jeans and was about to head upstairs to the Eagle's Nest Lounge to help rearrange the room for a large crowd to watch the football game—the opening event of the Christmas Eve celebration. Sadie sat at his feet, staring at him with adoring eyes.

"Are you going to have those pups pretty soon? Huh, girl?" He patted the top of her silky head. "You must feel better today." Did dogs have false labor? She sure acted like it last night, whining, pacing and clawing at her bed.

He finished putting on his shoes and stood up. Sadie sashayed toward the door and began to whine to go outside. He pulled the drapes back and looked out at the pool area. The room still sat empty with "Closed for Maintenance" signs around the room. Relieved, he opened the door and let the dog out.

"Come on, girl. Quick now..." They darted around the corner and down a short hallway to a side door. Ryan stayed inside while she dribbled on the snowy ground. She quickly came back to the door and clawed on the glass before he could get it open. He took her back to the room, made sure she had water and food then went to the bar.

He found Red busy giving orders to a small band of helpers. Ryan pitched in moving all of the sofas and easy chairs in front of the fireplace and filling the rest of the areas with long banquet tables. Once they finished their work in the bar, Red sent them all to The Pines ballroom to set up for the community buffet dinner after the game. There, Ryan found Katie working with Mandy and another group of volunteers setting up the circular tables and decorating them with white cloths and holiday centerpieces.

"We missed our lunch date," he said to Katie as he unfolded the legs on a large, round table and set it upright. "It was my fault and I apologize. Red had me so busy setting up the bar I lost track of the time."

"That's okay. I did, too," she said sweetly and

unfolded the tablecloth then spread it over the table. "There's a lot to do to get ready for tonight."

He walked over to a stack of banquet chairs and began pulling them apart. "The pre-game show is at one o'clock. Do you want to join me in the bar for some snacks and a glass of wine or a beer?"

She grabbed the chairs as he handed them to her and arranged them around the table. "I'd love to, but I signed up to coordinate the children's activities this afternoon."

They continued to work together with the other volunteers until they finished setting up the vast room. Ryan wished Katie would have accepted his invitation to spend the afternoon with him, but at the same time, he admired her for following her heart. The sparkle in her eyes and spring in her step demonstrated how much she enjoyed working on the events.

Once they finished setting up the tables, Ryan went back to the room to check on Sadie and take her outside to relieve herself. After that, he walked to the lobby to find Katie. He saw her reading "'Twas The Night Before Christmas" to a group of enthralled children and waved to her. "I'll meet you here after the game and walk you to dinner."

A couple young boys ran up to Katie to show her the snowmen they'd drawn on white paper and the scene reminded him of his twin nephews. He suddenly missed them. He missed them all—his sister, Beth and her husband, George, and he regretted taking out his anger over his parents' divorce on them by refusing their invitation to come for Christmas.

Determined to make it up to them when he got home, Ryan went into the gift shop to find some last-minute gifts for the boys.

The clerk behind the counter, dark-haired and slender, reminded him of Beth. "May I help you?"

"Yeah," Ryan said, looking around. "I need gifts for a couple of five-year-old boys. What would you suggest?"

The only toys left were ridiculously expensive, but Ryan saw something that caught his eye and immediately knew he'd found the perfect gift for Hunter and Hudson. He couldn't wait to see their faces when they opened their packages and found John Deere "Prestige" replica tractors with matching green and yellow John Deere bill caps.

While the clerk wrapped his purchases, Ryan searched for something to give to Katie. He found a hand-crocheted ski cap in the same light gray as her coat, but he wanted something more, something to match the sparkle in her eyes. He looked into the lighted jewelry case and saw the perfect item. "I'll take that, too," he said and pointed to a snowflake pin with sapphire and white crystal stones. The clerk wrapped the pin box with blue foil paper and a silver bow.

The pre-game show had already started by the time Ryan walked into The Eagle's Nest carrying his purchases in a large sack. So many people had come to watch the game he couldn't get near the bar, so he simply waved hello to Red and flagged the cocktail server on duty to order a beer. Despite the addition of more tables and chairs, Ryan could barely find an area to stand, much less a comfortable place to sit. He'd waited all day for this game, but oddly enough, now that it was about to start, he had no interest in it. He kept thinking about Katie and the gifts he planned to surprise her with tonight.

After a long wait, the cocktail server finally came back with his beer. He paid her for it and took a swig. *Meh...* He'd ordered his favorite brand, but today it tasted boring and flat. Ryan set the bottle on top of a covered trashcan and walked out.

Chapter Seven

Katie leaned over a long table in the lobby, helping a small girl cut out a paper snowflake. Someone approached her and the footsteps sounded familiar. She looked up.

"Ryan, what are you doing here?"

He stood before her, handsome in his red shirt and black jeans, smiling and holding a ridiculously large sack. "I got bored with the game. Need some help?"

"But...you were looking forward to it."

He shrugged. "I'd rather be with you."

Her jaw dropped slightly, but she quickly recovered and smiled back. "Okay. Do you want to cut snowflakes to tape on the wall or would you like to work with the older kids?"

At the next table, middle-grade children were having the time of their lives, frosting sugar cookies. Two of the older boys were working on assembling a gingerbread house.

Ryan nodded toward the cookie frosters. "I'll sit with them. The chairs are higher and I'm in the mood for a good old-fashioned Christmas cookie."

Katie pointed toward the sack. "What's that?"

He held it up. "Something I should have taken care of before I came up here."

Behind him, the gingerbread house collapsed and the boys groaned in frustration. "What's the matter, boys?" He set the bag under the table and pulled out a chair. "Let me show you how this is done..."

At five o'clock, Katie and Ryan met the girls in the ballroom for dinner. The NFL game ended about the same time and people were streaming into the room, filling up the tables. A retired pastor gave the blessing and announced a candlelight service in the chapel after dinner.

"Katie, are you going to the candlelight service?" Mandy asked as the group dined on baked chicken and mashed potatoes. "Susan and Nila are singing in the choir."

Susan and Nila glanced at each other and

blushed.

"We're not great singers," Nila said as she pulled apart a piece of buttered roll. "We just thought it would be fun."

"That sounds like a wonderful idea." Katie replied. She turned to Ryan. "How about you? Will you come, too?"

"I will on one condition," he said, frowning. "No one volunteers *me* to sing."

After dinner, they all went to the chapel. Pastor Howard's wife directed the small choir made up of guests and hotel staff. Katie sat with Ryan and Mandy while Susan and Nila took their places with the other singers in the front of the room. When the choir sang "O Holy Night," Ryan slid his arm around Katie and gave her a hug. She gazed into his deep brown eyes and found comfort in his presence. He wound his fingers around hers and whispered, "Merry Christmas, Katie."

Twenty-four hours ago, she wouldn't have believed it possible, but tonight she *was* having a merry Christmas.

After the service, Pastor Howard dismissed

everyone to attend the children's gift opening in the lobby. The girls disappeared, but Ryan and Katie went down to the lobby to watch Red say "Ho, ho, ho!" and hand out gifts in his Santa suit.

"This is one show I've got to see," Ryan remarked with a wry grin as they walked into the lobby.

Red looked impressive in his Santa suit and white cotton beard. When he greeted the children and jiggled his fake belly, his blue eyes danced with merriment, just like the real Santa. Unfortunately, some of the children, mostly the very young ones, were afraid of his red suit and booming voice. They cried when their parents tried to set them on his lap.

"*Help*," he mouthed to Ryan as one of the parents pulled a screaming baby off his knee.

Katie and Ryan turned away and burst out laughing.

"Poor Red!" Katie said, feeling guilty for finding his predicament funny. "We'd better do something to help him."

She went to the Christmas tree and began pulling out gifts for Santa to give to the kids. The atmosphere changed immediately as the older children clustered around him with excitement.

They were handing out the last few packages when Mandy raced into the lobby. "Ryan! Ryan! Hurry, it's time!"

~*~

Ryan knelt next to Sadie and stroked the back of her neck. "It's going to be okay, girl."

The girls had pulled the loveseat away from Sadie's box so everyone could be near the dog. Ryan stared up at Nila. "Are you sure she's ready to have her pups? How do you know?"

Nila knelt next to him. "She's dilated."

Ryan blinked. "She's what?"

Nila showed him the area. "This tells me her body is getting ready for delivery." She gently patted Sadie on the back. "I can't say exactly when, but I think she's going to discharge her first one very soon. She's having contractions." Nila twisted her shoulder-length dark hair into a knot and wound an elastic band around it. "This process is going to take a while, so we might as well get comfortable."

Ryan stared at her feeling completely helpless.

"Like, how long?"

"I don't know. Each pup will come at its own pace. Some may come ten minutes apart, but others might take an hour or longer."

Ryan ran his hands through his hair and stood up. An hour or longer? At that rate, it could take all night. He joined Katie on the loveseat and sat back, closing his eyes. The process had barely begun and he was already exhausted. He sighed with gratitude, relieved the girls were eager to help.

Katie looked up from researching canine labor and delivery videos on her laptop. "Let's put on some music to help Sadie relax." She put her computer aside and went to the radio on the nightstand. She found a local radio station playing Christmas music and turned the volume down to a pleasant hum as an instrumental rendition of "The Little Drummer Boy" came on.

Everyone began to yawn.

Susan climbed to her feet. "We need some caffeine or we're never going to last. I'll make some coffee." She brewed a pot and gave a cup to each person except Mandy, who had almost immediately fallen asleep on the floor. Susan spread a blanket over Mandy then sat next to Sadie's box to wait it out.

Katie went into the bathroom to gather a stack of hand towels. "I have to get some dental floss," she said when she came back and set the towels next to the whelping box. "It's for tying off the umbilical cord." She zipped open her suitcase and pulled out what she needed.

Within the hour, Sadie began to whine and push hard. Everyone gathered around her to witness the birth of her first pup. Katie spoke to Sadie in a soothing voice and gently stroked her back.

"Oh, my gosh, here it comes," Susan said, folding her hands together as though she had a mind to pray.

Ryan kneeled and watched as the pup's black head emerged. He marveled at its tiny pink nose and mouth. "Come on, girl. One more push. You can do it." Suddenly the pup's body jetted out encased in a filmy sac, followed by a rush of fluids.

Everyone cheered the pup's arrival.

"Good girl," Ryan said and wondered how many more times he would end up repeating that line.

He stared with fascination as Katie picked up the pup and wrapped it in a towel. She made a hole in the birth sac with her fingernail and rubbed the film off the pup with the towel's soft fabric. Then she tenderly cleaned its tiny, square face.

Sadie watched the entire process and now nudged her nose over the little black pup's soft, wet body. Once she had inspected her firstborn, she began gently washing it with her tongue.

"She's massaging the pup to stimulate breathing and improve its circulation," Katie said. "She's also bonding with it."

They waited until Sadie bit off the umbilical cord then Katie took an eight-inch string of dental floss and tied off the piece of cord still attached to the pup's body.

Nila held up her phone. "I want to get a picture of you guys holding the first one." Katie moved close to Ryan and held the pup between their faces.

Nila emailed the picture to Ryan as Katie placed the pup at Sadie's tummy to nurse.

A half-hour later, puppy number two came

through the birth canal.

"Oh, look," Katie exclaimed and pointed toward the puppy's markings. "This one is black and white."

"Ryan, it's your turn," Susan said.

Everyone looked at him, waiting for him to get with the program.

"No way," he said, going into panic mode. He held up his hands as he stood up and backed away. "I don't know anything about delivering babies."

"It's easy," Katie said quietly and touched his arm. "Sadie does all the work. All you have to do is wipe off the film."

At her word, he nervously picked up a towel and watched for the newborn to emerge. Once it appeared, however, he forgot his apprehension when Katie pierced the birth sac for him and placed the pup in his hand. "It has that new puppy smell," he said, captivated by the tiny body nestled in his palm as he gently wiped it clean.

Susan's turn came with puppy number three and Nila's turn came with the one after that.

An hour went by before puppy number five

came into the world. By four o'clock in the morning Sadie was the proud mother of four solid black pups and four black and white "parti-colored" pups.

Chapter Eight

"We need to monitor Sadie for a couple hours to make sure there are no more pups coming," Katie said quietly as she rubbed her eyes, "but I'm so tired I don't think I can stay awake that long."

Susan had already fallen asleep on the floor next to Mandy. Nila sat on one of the beds, struggling to keep her eyes open.

"We need some fresh air," Ryan said and stood up. He grabbed a couple bottles of water and held out his hand. "Come on, let's go for a walk."

Katie snatched her purse, checking first to make sure she had his gift tucked inside before following him out the door.

They walked quietly through the pool area into the hallway, slipped past the people sleeping in the lobby and made their way upstairs to the Eagle's Nest Lounge.

She looked around. Most of the lights were off, but one small light shined behind the bar. "Where are we going?" she whispered.

Ryan pointed toward the sunken living room area. "This is the only place I know of where we can talk without bothering anyone or having our conversation overheard." He held her hand as she descended the steps and led her to a sofa in front of the darkened fireplace.

"Have a seat. I'll be right back." She watched in puzzlement as he set the bottles of water on a coffee table and walked over to a panel of electrical switches on the wall. He tested each one until a small flame flickered in the fireplace.

He came back and sat down beside her. "Let's have a toast." He opened both of the water bottles and handed her one. "Here's to a few minutes of peace and quiet." They touched their bottles together and drank the water.

"I've wanted to give this to you since yesterday afternoon." Ryan pulled a small box wrapped in blue foil and garnished with a silver bow from the pocket of his shirt and placed it in her hand. "Merry Christmas, Katie."

She tore off the paper and opened the box. The pin sparkled against the flames now glowing in the fireplace. "Oh, Ryan, it's beautiful," she said, keeping her voice low. "Thank you. It will look perfect on my coat."

Ryan reached into his back pocket and pulled out another package, narrow and flat. "This goes with it." He set it in her lap. "I thought it would look nice on you."

Knowing he'd picked out the items with such care warmed her heart. She tore off the paper, but when she saw the contents, she began to quiver with silent laughter.

His smile faded into an expression of alarm. "What's wrong? Don't you like it?"

"Oh, Ryan, it's perfect!" She reached into her purse and pulled out a similar-looking gift in the same blue wrapping paper. "This is for you."

He pulled the paper open and held up the gray ski cap.

They burst into laughter as they each pulled on their caps.

Ryan moved close. "I like the sound of your laughter, Katie. It's sweet, like you." He traced the contour of her cheek with his thumb. "You're so pretty when you smile. I like making you smile and I'm glad being with me makes you happy."

Katie gazed into his eyes and realized he was right. He did make her smile and she suddenly knew why. Except for one conversation, she hadn't thought about Josh since Friday night when she walked into the Eagle's Nest hauling her suitcase and literally slammed into Ryan. She hadn't forgotten about Josh. He'd always hold a special place in her heart. Rather, she'd simply chosen to focus on the present instead of dwelling on the past.

"I am happy," she whispered, aware that choosing to let go of her grieving had lifted a huge burden from her soul. "I thought coming back here would crush me. Instead I've become stronger because I had to face my fear and now I'm grateful it happened." She gave him a heartfelt smile. "Thank you for being a caring friend."

"Katie, I want to be more," he whispered and slid his long, muscular arms around her waist, pulling her close. He held her gently at first, cheek to cheek, as though gauging her response. The strength of his arms comforted her, giving her an innate sense of his trust and protectiveness. She relaxed and inhaled a deep breath. The spicy aroma of his aftershave filled her head, sharpening her senses.

He angled his head and tenderly brushed her lips, but deepened the pressure as she wrapped her arms around his neck and pulled him closer, matching the intensity of his kiss. She had long forgotten the anticipation and excitement of new love, but the warmth of his mouth upon hers reawakened her passion and made her realize the depth of her loneliness. How much she'd missed by looking back instead of forging ahead.

He leaned her back against the pillows on the sofa, reclining her in a half-sitting position. "The moment I saw you, I wondered what it would be like to hold you in my arms and kiss you," he said softly. "You were crying because you couldn't get your car to drive off the ice. I took one look in your eyes and knew I'd push your car to Alaska if you asked me to." He chuckled and kissed her again. And again.

"I'd like to see you after Christmas," he said and toyed with a strand of her hair. "Perhaps we could go out to dinner and take in a movie—"

Ryan stopped and listened, his attention

focused on the emotional outburst of voices downstairs. He stood up. "Did you hear that? Someone just said the storm is over."

Katie jumped off the sofa and followed Ryan to the wall of windows on the other side of the lounge. They wouldn't see the sunrise for another hour, but already the sky seemed to be getting lighter. She stood at the window and stared out at the lighted grounds of the resort and the frozen lake. The wind had indeed subsided.

"I'm going home today," Katie said slowly, her heart conflicted by the thought. She couldn't wait to get back to Minneapolis and have Christmas dinner with her family, but at the same time, going home meant she'd be leaving Ryan. She looked at him and suddenly wished the snow would have continued for one more day.

"We'd better get downstairs and see what's going on." Ryan sounded excited as he led the way back to the living room to collect their things. Katie grabbed her purse, her snowflake pin and the water bottles while Ryan shut off the fireplace. She followed him out of the bar, tossing the wrapping in the trash on her way out.

Downstairs, jubilant pandemonium reigned as people began to wake up and get ready to leave. The aromas of fresh brewed coffee and cinnamon rolls drifted from the snack bar. Ryan and Katie hurried to his room and found the girls sound asleep, still in the same places they'd been when she left.

"Mandy, Susan, Nila, get up," Katie said as she began to turn on the lights and collect her things. The girls stirred, voicing groans of protest. "The storm is over. You can go home!"

"W-h-a-a-a-t?" Mandy sat up on the carpet and rubbed her eyes. "I need some coffee first."

Katie grabbed the coffee pot. "I'll make some."

"N-o-o-o-o," she complained. "I want some *good* coffee."

Nila pulled the blanket over her head. "I'm so tired..."

"You're tired?" Katie laughed. "I haven't even been to bed yet."

Ryan stomped around the room, turning over boxes and tossing clothes out of his closet. "Where's my jacket? I'm going out for a ride." Katie helped him look for it, but they couldn't find it anywhere. How could a bright red jacket disappear?

"Maybe I left it in the bar yesterday." He pulled a down vest out of the closet and slid his arms into it. "See you later," he said and headed for the door.

Katie pulled her wallet out of her purse and followed him. "I'm going to the snack bar to get everyone some coffee."

In the lobby, Ryan grabbed Katie around the waist and gave her a kiss. "Don't leave until I get back."

Katie stood in line at the snack bar and watched him leave knowing the spring in his step had to do with more than just a fast ride over fresh powder. At the same time, a part of her worried about his safety on his sled—given her tragic past, she couldn't help it—but from what she knew of Ryan already, she believed he was a skilled, sensible driver and she forced herself to put her worries aside.

Twenty minutes later, she arrived back at the room. The girls were lying in the beds under the covers now, still half-asleep.

"Sorry it took so long. The line at the snack bar stretched almost to the front door. They ran out of coffee twice." She handed out extra large cups to the girls. "I bought a bag of caramel rolls, too. The frosted cinnamon rolls were already gone."

Susan sat up and blew on her coffee. "I'll bet you're happy to get out of here," she said and slurped the hot liquid.

Katie sat on the bed and pulled the top off her cup. "Not as much as I thought I would."

Nila poked one eye open. "Are you going to see Ryan again after you get back to Minneapolis?"

Katie smiled and slipped her hand into the bag with a paper napkin for a sticky caramel roll. "Yeah." She bit into the roll and added with her mouth full of sticky caramel, "He's taking me out to dinner."

"O-o-o-o-o-h," they said in unison.

Mandy sat up and reached for the bag of rolls. "I knew you two would get together. You're made for each other."

Katie walked over to Sadie's bed and kissed her on the top of the head. Someone had put her red collar on and attached a small red velvet bow to it. She lifted Ryan's red jacket covering the puppies and found them huddled on top of each other, sound asleep. She lowered the jacket back down, not wanting them to get cold.

So...that's what happened to his jacket. At least it disappeared for a good cause.

A half-hour later, Katie hugged each girl goodbye after "friending" them on Facebook. She petted Sadie and rolled her suitcase to the lobby. She planned to haul it out to her car and clean off the snow before Ryan came back. They needed to exchange phone numbers and email addresses and talk about his plans for the dog. She assumed he'd take the dog home, but she wanted to know more.

She pulled her suitcase through the front doors and stood in the crisp, clear morning, gazing at the snow. The maintenance crew had already cleared half of the parking lot and she breathed a sigh of relief to see that it was *her* half. She rolled her suitcase out to her car. The howling of dozens of snowmobiles racing past the resort filled the atmosphere on this sunny, but peaceful day.

She came upon an older car and recognized

Maggie leaning across the back seat, buckling Logan into his safety seat. "Merry Christmas!" Katie said with a wave as she passed by.

Maggie stood up, smiling. "Merry Christmas, to you, too! Thank you again for the wonderful room!"

Katie stood brushing a mountain of snow off her car, enjoying the sunshine when she saw Ryan drive his Polaris toward a red Silverado pickup truck with a large covered trailer hitched to the back. At first, she shuddered at the thought of even getting near his snowmobile, but deep in her soul, a still, small voice urged her to let go of her fear. She used to love the freedom of racing across open fields and hitting the trails with Josh. Ever since his accident, though, she'd avoided all contact with the sport.

Still, what happened to Josh was tragic, but rare. He had the misfortune to be in the wrong place at the wrong time. As a former owner of a Polaris herself, she knew most people who possessed snowmobiles were responsible and used common sense. Ryan's machine looked new and had a lot of power, and based upon her own experience, she could tell he handled it well.

I can't evade the issue forever. If I'm going to date someone who loves the sport, I need to deal with my fear...

She finished cleaning off her car and trudged through the snow to Ryan's truck.

His Polaris sat next to his trailer, cooling down—the key still in the ignition.

"Ryan," Katie called out as she walked around the truck, looking for him. "Ryan, where are you?"

He didn't answer.

She walked back to his sled and stood next to it, wondering what it would be like to get on the back of it, slide her arms around Ryan's waist and go with him for a short ride. Her heart skipped a beat at the thought of sitting at the controls and driving it herself. Tentatively, she placed her hand on the seat, ready to jump back at any moment if the machine decided to flip over on her.

But it didn't move. It didn't make a sound. It simply sat there like an obedient steed, waiting for her to give it a command.

Willing herself to move past her fear, she squared her shoulders and slid her leg over the beast, easing herself down on the seat. Her hands automatically gripped the handlebars. Then something unexpected happened. Memories of driving her own sled came back in a rush—the force of the machine thundering underneath her, trees and hills flying by, the wind on her face...

Curious, she checked the brake, the engine stop switch and the choke. The only thing left to do was...turn the key. She sat there for a moment and debated.

Should I?

The crash site wasn't far away. She could make it there in less than five minutes and come right back. The urge to face the scene of Josh's death once more and put the tragedy behind her fueled her decision.

She started the machine, released the choke and took off. Her hands shook as she drove the sled out of the parking lot toward a snow-covered road that led to the trail that would take her to the place where the accident happened. It didn't take long before her instincts took over and she began to calm down.

The road came upon three trails. Katie veered

off on the middle one and headed for the place where the road wound back and crossed the trail again—the place where Josh lost his life. She rounded the bend and slowed down. The crash scene loomed in the distance but when she arrived, she barely recognized it. Everything had changed.

She stopped the snowmobile and looked around in shock. The resort had removed many of the trees and shrubs and leveled the land to make room for a new development of timeshare units. Likewise, the trail no longer crossed the road. The maintenance crew had rerouted it in different direction, detouring snowmobile traffic away from the area.

Nothing looked the same.

It's as though it never happened here, Katie thought, realizing all that physically remained of that day existed only in the images stored in her memory. *Everyone has moved on.*

She thought about how many times she'd revisited the scene in her head and knew she didn't want her grief to define her as a person any longer.

Josh will always hold a special place in my heart, but I need to move on, too.

She turned the sled around and raced back to the parking lot, anxious to tell Ryan what she'd found.

Chapter Nine

Ryan paced back and forth in the snow, his temper on the verge of exploding. He stopped in front of a pair of guys who'd supposedly saw the thief steal his Polaris. "Are you sure you saw a *woman* driving off in my sled?"

The shorter one in a black jacket and snow pants nodded. "Bout this high, wearing a light coat."

"Did you see her face? Catch a description?"

The men shook their heads.

"She was gone before we could get a good look," the man said. "Started 'er right up and flew outta here. Knew what she was doin', I tell ya."

Ryan picked up his phone and had begun dialing 9-1-1 when he heard a familiar deep whine and looked up. He nearly dropped his phone before he literally saw red—his red Polaris with Katie at the controls, driving toward him.

He didn't even wait for her to stop before he

came toward her shaking his fist in the air. "What do you think you're doing, taking my sled without asking my permission?"

"I'm sorry, Ryan." She turned it off and looked startled by his show of anger. "I called your name several times. Where did you—"

"Where I went doesn't matter! Where did *you* go?"

"Well, that's what I want to tell you about—"

"You almost gave me a heart attack, Katie. I thought someone had stolen my new sled right from under my nose." He shook his finger in her face. "Don't *ever* do that again! Do you understand? I almost reported you to the police."

The corners of her mouth tightened. "Look, I said I'm sorry. You're right. I should have asked you first. I didn't mean to make you upset, Ryan. It's just that I—I simply wanted to see if I could get on a snowmobile and drive it back to the scene of the accident."

"That's ridiculous. Why didn't you wait for me? You told me you haven't been on one in two years. You could have crashed it and become a fatality yourself. Promise me you'll never do something so foolish again!"

"It was something I needed to do myself!" she shouted and hopped off the Polaris. "Don't worry. I'll never ride on your stupid sled again!"

She turned her back on him and stormed away, heading back to the hotel.

Still upset, Ryan drove his sled into his trailer and locked it up. Then he drove his pickup to the side door by his room and went in to get the dog.

On the way in, he passed the hotel manager, Mr. Jameson.

"I see you've pulled your vehicle up to the building, blocking the entrance. That's against the fire code, but I'll let it go because I assume you're checking out," Mr. Jameson said as they approached each other in the pool area. He stopped and placed his hands on his hips with a no-nonsense glare in his eyes. "Make sure you take that *dog* with you."

Ryan's temper had cooled considerably by the time he walked into his room and found Susan, Mandy and Nila sitting on the floor, each holding a puppy.

"I'm checking out," he said and began stuffing items into his duffel bag. He stopped next to the loveseat, lifting one brow at the sight of his red jacket covering the dog's box.

Mandy's face went into instant panic mode at his statement and she exchanged worried glances with her friends. She stood up, holding a black puppy to her cheek. "What about Sadie? She can't stay in this room once you're gone."

"I'm taking her home with me."

Mandy burst into tears.

What the...

Ryan placed his hands on his hips. "Hey, isn't that what you wanted? To find a home for her?"

"Yes, but we're going to miss her," Susan said, her voice heavy with emotion. She held up a black and white puppy in front of her face. "And her sweet little babies."

Nila stood up. "Do you promise to take excellent care of Sadie and find good homes for the puppies?"

"Of course I will," he said. "It just so happens my house has a fenced-in backyard because the former owner had kids and I know a few people who will take a puppy." His sister, for one. Hunter and Hudson needed a dog to play with.

He decided to keep his jacket as a cover for Sadie's box and set it on the bed. "Come here, girl," he said gently and hooked the leash onto her collar. "I'll carry the box out to my truck and put it in the back seat, but I need one of you to follow me with Sadie."

"I'll do it," Mandy said and slipped the puppy in her hands back into the box. Susan and Nila followed her lead and returned theirs as well.

"Goodbye, Sadie," Susan said and began to sob as she petted the dog. "We'll miss you."

Then Mandy and Nila began to cry and Ryan knew he had to get out of there. He picked up the whelping box and started for the door. Sadie strained at her leash, whining for her pups.

He winced with guilt at the sound of Sadie's whimpering, but his reaction to the dog's emotion was nothing compared to the remorse he carried over yelling at Katie.

~*~

Katie wiped away tears with the backs of her hands as she walked back to her car. She'd gone to the restroom to cool down and wash her face, only to start crying again. Ryan had hurt her feelings, but she knew he had every right to be upset when he discovered his sled gone and thought someone had stolen it.

You know better than that. You should have stuck around until he came back. No one takes off on a person's sled without asking...

She'd planned to apologize, this time sincerely, and set things straight between them again, but when she walked out to the parking area, Ryan's pickup truck and trailer had disappeared. She made a 360 degree turn—twice—and couldn't spot his red truck and trailer anywhere.

He left! I made him so angry he simply left!

Numb with shock, she climbed into her car and started it up. She let it warm up a little and drove out of the parking lot believing she would never see The Lakewood Resort or Ryan Scott again.

~*~

Ryan's heart sunk as he drove back to the guest

parking lot and found an empty spot where Katie's Malibu once sat. She'd left without saying goodbye.

He knew he shouldn't have lost his temper, but when he saw her driving toward him on his sled, he realized how deeply it would affect him if anything serious ever happened to her. It scared him to think she'd go out on his Polaris without him along, at least the first time, anyway. He didn't care if she drove it once she'd had a refresher course and some practice. In fact, he'd be more than happy to help her find the right sled if she wanted her own.

He pulled out his phone and stared at the photo Nila had emailed to him, captivated by the sparkle in Katie's eyes and her beautiful smile. She no longer resembled the tearful, stressed-out woman he'd first met. She had changed. He had changed, too—because of her.

Ryan smacked his hand against the steering wheel, realizing he couldn't even call her to try to make things right. He'd planned to get her phone number and program it into his phone before they left, but never got the chance.

Maybe I can catch up to her. I don't know if she'll even pull over, much less talk to me, but I have to try.

He pulled out of the resort and drove toward the freeway past huge drifts and snow-covered secondary roads. The snowplows had cleared the main road, but nothing else. He stared straight ahead, concentrating on getting to I-94 and finding Katie.

Ryan found the exit ramp open and drove cautiously onto the freeway. He didn't see Katie's car up ahead, but that didn't deter him. He had several hours to catch up with her.

By the time he reached St. Cloud, however, Ryan had begun to wonder how he could have missed her. He pulled into a large gas station and convenience store to fill up his tank...and pulled right in behind Katie's Malibu.

She stood at the pump, feeding her credit card to the machine to fill her car. Her jaw dropped when she saw him pull in and stop right behind her.

Nervous he'd screw up again, he jumped out of the vehicle and walked toward her. "I'm sorry Katie," he blurted the moment their gazes met. "I didn't mean to make you upset."

"I'm sorry, Ryan," she said at the same time. "I should never have taken off on your sled without talking to you first."

"I'm over it." He took the nozzle from her hand, stuck it in the Malibu's gas tank, squeezed the trigger and set the automatic shut-off valve. Then he leaned over and kissed her. "And to prove it to you, I'm giving you permission to take it any time you want."

"Are you sure? I'm going to hold you to it."

"Yeah. When do you want to take it for a practice spin?"

"I'd take you up on it right now if I could." She leaned against the car with one gloved hand. The snowflake pin he'd given her looked as pretty on her coat as he'd imagined it would. "Where are you going? I thought you wanted to spend a few days at the resort," she said, "especially now that there is so much fresh powder on the ground."

"I've changed my mind," he said and looked into her eyes. "I'm going to surprise my sister and show up for dinner with my gifts for the boys. Besides, you said you'd have dinner with me when we get back. I'm thinking tomorrow night." He kissed her again. "What about you? Did you call your parents and tell them you're on your way?"

She laughed. "I forgot I'd turned off my phone yesterday. When I talked to them they were upset that I didn't answer their calls and hadn't called them."

He put his hand on her chin and pulled her close. "You were busy delivering puppies."

She put her hands to her face. "Oh, my gosh! What about Sadie? What happened to her?"

He gestured toward the truck. "She's in the back seat with her pups. I'm bringing her home with me, but I don't know what I'm going do with nine dogs roaming around my house. Do you want a pup in about two months?"

Her eyes sparkled with amusement as she placed her hands on his shoulders. "You bet I do, but I plan to be around much longer than that."

He pulled her into his arms and kissed her, sealing the deal.

A Note from the Author

Thank you for reading my novella, "A CHRISTMAS TO REMEMBER." I love animals and they always seem to find their way into my stories. Sadie is near and dear to my heart because she was a real dog that I had for fifteen years. She was only half Cocker Spaniel and the other half was anybody's guess, but I think it might have been rat terrier. She was black and had a lot of long, wavy hair. When my sister rescued her from an animal shelter, Sadie was pregnant and close to giving birth. Lori said she fell in love with Sadie because of her big, sad eyes. Sadie was a sweet dog who will always have a place in my heart and one day I will meet her again at the edge of the Rainbow Bridge.

If you enjoyed this novel, I would appreciate it if you would tell other readers about it by recommending it and reviewing it on line. If you would like more information about me or my other books, I have provided the information on the next page.

Other Books by Denise Devine

Merry Christmas, Darling – A sweet, romantic comedy

This Time Forever – An inspirational romance

Romance and Mystery Under the Northern Lights – An anthology of short stories

Contact Information

Denise's Website:

www.deniseannettedevine.com

Facebook Author Page:

www.facebook.com/deniseannettedevine

www.facebook.com/groups/SRRCafe1/

Pinterest Page:

www.pinterest.com/denisedevine1

Amazon Author Page:
www.amazon/com/author/denisedevine

Made in the USA
Charleston, SC
15 October 2016